UNGODLY

Tate Dousette

DARK MYTH
www.darkmythpublications.com

Dark Myth Publications
145 S Glenoaks Blvd.
Unit #3149,
Burbank, CA 91502

ISBN: 979-8-9925038-9-0
First Printing November 2025

Dark Myth Publications is a registered trademark of The JayZoMon Dark Myth Company, LLC.

10 9 8 7 6 5 4 3 2 1

Table of Contents

UNGODLY

CHAPTER 1
THE FALL FROM HEAVEN

IT WAS THE summer of 1995 somewhere along the strip of downtown Los Angeles. The brothers' bicentennial excursion to Earth was proceeding splendidly. Hermes and Apollo, disguised in washed pastel leisure suits just a season or two out of style, carelessly sipped cocktails as they fraternized with mortals in a local hole-in-the-wall joint. Red noses and glazed eyes crowded into the dimly lit bar like canned sardines. Cigarette smoke drifted throughout the room, pairing well with the stench of clammy desperation. Patron's drunken laughter and half-witted small talk engulfed the soft beach Indie music humming dully through a stereo located in the corner by a pool table. The brothers relaxed in the corner booth beside it so they could enjoy the new music as well as a friendly pool game. Hermes was busy flirting with yet another patron, while it was Apollo's turn to shoot.

"I must say, women in Los Angeles are quite lovely. You have eyes as piercing as a sword, my dear." Hermes quipped.

The woman giggled as her face flushed to a bright pink tone. "Heh, kind of an odd compliment, but I guess anything sounds hot with that accent."

Hermes chuckled as he twirled his finger through his luscious, permed brunette curls. "It's funny to think how much the language has changed over the years."

The woman stared at Hermes as if she couldn't look away, completely entranced. She questioned in her head if he were in fact the most beautiful man she'd ever seen. "So where are you from with an accent like that?" She leaned closer towards him, her heart beating slightly quicker now.

Hermes casually stirred the toothpick puncturing through the green olive garnishing his glass. "Well, Greece, originally. Now I'm living much higher in altitude." Hermes couldn't help but smirk at his own response.

She tilted her head, perplexed, "You sound more British than Greek."

Hermes sipped his martini and shrugged, though he was in fact speaking with a British accent. Truth be told, during one of the brothers' past visits down to earth, they went to London, becoming so infatuated by British accents that they began speaking with them. This struck neither of them as distasteful nor even odd for that matter. Hermes changed the subject. "And are you from the land of Los Angeles?"

The curly-haired bar patron sipped her drink, sure not to smear the gloss of lipstick coating her lips. "Well, originally I'm from Wisconsin, but I wanted somewhere with more sunshine, y'know?"

Hermes grinned mischievously before pointing his thumb back towards Apollo. "Ah yes, well you should talk to my brother if it's the sun you're looking for!" He excitedly waved him over. The brothers had a pompous tendency to show off. They obviously thought this to be charming, though even the other Gods on Olympus found it obnoxious. "Brother, this fair maiden is quite a fan of the sun. Would you care to show her a trick?"

Apollo basked in a smug, self-obsessed grin before setting his pool cue down. He leisurely swayed his lanky, broad-shouldered frame towards the woman, sure to take his sweet time with each step before finally gracing her with his presence. He leaned in close, held one hand out in front of her, and snapped his finger, making a flame ignite from his fingertip.

The woman let out an involuntary yelp of excitement followed by drunken giggles. "Oh wow, that's some party trick! How did you even do that?"

Apollo casually blew the flame out atop his fingertip. "That, my dear, is a secret only for the Gods." He pulled his small, circular-framed sunglasses down and winked at the woman.

Hermes fidgeted in his seat, becoming bored of the conversation. He was much more interested in scoping out what souvenir he would bring home with him this visit. The God of Thievery had accrued quite the collection from his past outings to the mortal realm. The souvenirs ranged anywhere from the crowns of past kings to the famously unrecovered painting "The Concert" by Johannes Vermeer. Though, this time he was looking for something with a little less flash. This time, he wanted something that represented the common mortal. Finally something had caught his eye: the square, pocket-sized leather folder that held the mortal's currency. *Perfect*, he thought. The curly-haired trickster conveniently swished the olive and half-melted ice cube around the bottom of his glass. "I'm going to grab another one of those martinis; I have become quite fond of them!"

Apollo waved his brother away. "Take your time!" The platinum-haired Adonis only paid half attention to his brother, as he was preoccupied bragging about himself to the woman.

Hermes walked to the bar, curiously watching all the mortals around him as he began to ponder a realization. *It's quite different than I remember; even in just these past few years, mortals have changed far more than I ever thought they could...*

Just then Hermes met with the shoulder of a shorter but much heavier-set bar patron. He was a bearded gentleman, and it wouldn't take a detective to figure this man's occupation was most likely that of a truck driver. He jeered back at Hermes as he passed him. "Watch it, tears for queers."

Hermes turned around and mischievously cocked an eyebrow. He hadn't planned exactly which mortal's wallet he would steal yet. Though, for the cunning god, he never ceased to answer when an opportunity came knocking. "I beg your pardon?"

The stout trucker took this as a sign of aggression, turning back around and stepping closer towards Hermes' perfectly chiseled face. "I said watch it!"

With a sultry flick of his gaze, the corners of Hermes's lips curled into a seductive little grin, eyeing him up and down. Appraising the stranger as if he were a used car, and he was more than willing to take him for a test drive. "I must say you're not typically my type, but I'd be willing to make an exception."

"Don't get fucking smart with me, bud!" The trucker poked Hermes in the chest, taking another step closer.

Hermes let out a lighthearted sigh. He playfully chuckled and began to back up. It's no secret the god could hurl this mortal down into the depths of Tartarus if he wished to, though he didn't want to bring any unnecessary attention to him and his brother, as it could risk their father finding out about their occasional earthly outings. "My apologies, I didn't intend to upset you." Hermes patted him on the shoulder and began to walk away, subtly slipping the man's wallet inside his pant pocket. *Mortals were so slow,* he thought.

Unfortunately, about two steps later, the sound of leather slapping tile alerted the round, bearded man. He turned around, beet red in the face. "Hey! That's my wallet, asshole!"

Hermes sighed to himself. "Damn loose pockets…"

"Get your ass back here!" The trucker look-alike

5

rushed towards Hermes as he hastily attempted to make his escape.

Hermes darted over to his brother, nudging him in an attempt to get his attention, though Apollo was now busy flirting with a different woman. Hermes called out to him as loud as he could without further making a scene, similar to a mother scolding her child in a grocery store. "Brother!" He hissed. The God of the Sun attempted to shoo him away, but Hermes persisted. "Apollo!"

With a scowl now upon his face, Apollo turned towards his younger brother in annoyance. "What is it?"

Hermes looked uncharacteristically nervous; a cold sweat broke out across his forehead as he darted his eyes back at the stocky man, flaring his nostrils at him, now only a few feet away. *We can't risk making a scene*, he thought. "We have to go now." He implored his brother to see the severity of the situation.

Apollo failed to realize the sense of urgency, or maybe he just didn't care. He had been known to do both quite often. Like most Gods, Apollo only had one primary concern: pleasure. "In just a moment, I'm having fun."

Frustrated by his brother's self-centered antics, Hermes pinched his brow until the imprints of his fingers were etched on his nose. A vein pulsated in the center of his forehead. "We don't have time!"

Just then the bearded man's voice boomed behind them. "Hey! Get back here with my fucking wallet!" The man aggressively approached the two brothers.

Apollo stepped in front of Hermes; his brawny frame covered his brother completely. He stepped towards the red-faced, bearded man almost in excitement. If it weren't for the amount of alcohol the man consumed prior to the altercation, perhaps he would've noticed how much the God towered over him. The God of Light glared down at him menacingly. "Any quarrel you hold with my brother, you hold with me."

"Listen, prick, your butt buddy stole my wallet. So step aside, or I'll kick your ass too!" The trucker crassly slurred his words to the God of Light, all while aggressively pointing at Hermes.

Apollo had always been prideful. This oftentimes got either himself or someone else into trouble. With too many of those times ending in the abrupt skinning or immolation of a mortal.

"Prick?" The bottom lid of his left eye began to twitch up and down involuntarily as if he were short-circuiting. "You dare call me such insults? You *DARE* threaten *ME?*" Apollo began to glow golden as he shook with rage. Flames flared off his bronzed skin in a blaze of fury.

"Brother, no! We can't bring any more attention!" Hermes pleaded as he attempted to pull Apollo away, though the force of the God was too much now; there was no stopping the power yet to be released upon the pitifully inebriated and ignorant mortal.

Apollo was no longer listening to Hermes at this point. His eyes were as white as the stars, and the ends of his platinum blond hair flickered with flames. A golden aura radiated from him, momentarily blinding most of the other bar patrons. "My brother may have stolen your wallet, mere mortal, but I will steal your life!" With the touch of his palm to the man's face, Apollo ignited him into a burst of flames, which roared for only a second before vanishing into a pile of ash.

The other bar patrons screamed in horror, though most of them were too drunk or distraught to really grasp what had just happened. They just knew they were scared, and it now smelled of burning flesh throughout the bar.

Hermes sternly tugged his brother's arm towards the door. "We need to leave now!"

Apollo nodded, and the two ran out of the bar, soaring into the night sky back towards Olympus. Hermes spent the short flight home sternly scolding his brother for his actions.

Hermes yelled at his brother through the howling winds. "You shouldn't have done that; that is just the type of thing that can get back to Father!"

Apollo casually brushed off his brother's worries. "Relax, he doesn't pay any attention to what goes on down here." He always thought Hermes sometimes tended to be a stick in the mud.

Hermes tilted his head, looking at his brother like he had achieved a new level of stupidity. "You don't think he has spies? Creatures sent down to watch over here? It's still his domain, brother."

Apollo rolled his eyes at his brother's words, thinking no weight was behind them. He thought his brother was just anxious about getting caught, like he'd been on every other bicentennial excursion. "You're too paranoid. I only burnt one man alive in a room full of drunk people. I'm sure I blinded them all anyway."

Hermes sighed; his breath shook in the night sky as they approached the towering palace in the clouds bordering Earth's orbit. "I hope you're right, brother. I hope you're right…"

***

The two arrived back at Olympus, acting as if they'd been there all along. Once atop a mountain, the entirety of the golden utopia was on the brink of Earth's atmosphere now. As well as outlawing contact with mortals, Zeus raised all of Olympus into the skies, cloaking it with a storm only bearable to immortals. Palaces of the gods floated through the clouds around them as they walked into the main courtyard. White marbled columns towered around the perimeter, while the stars twinkled in between them. Matching marbled pathways accented with pockets of golden berry bushes led to the gods' palaces. A large and lavish meander-shaped fountain sat in the center of the courtyard, pouring water back and forth in an endless stream. A silver-haired Goddess stood by the infinite fountain, nervously awaiting her siblings' arrival.

A short turquoise robe hung over her body with a silver shining bow and quiver gleaming from her back. Her fair, phantom-like skin radiated off the stars as her chopped shaggy locks flowed perfectly with the night breeze. Her eyes glittered brighter than the moon itself.

She was the moon itself, and her brother the sun. Artemis was the polar opposite of her twin brother Apollo. She was the brains to his brawn before Hermes came along, though she didn't mind her half-brother's arrival. Artemis loved her twin brother, but he could be a bit much at times. She was much more grounded than Apollo, oftentimes being the more clear-headed one of the two. Don't be fooled; if aggravated enough, she was known to share her brother's temper.

Hermes and Apollo approached the goddess. Hermes shared the same concerned expression as her, though Apollo only obliviously grinned and rushed to hug his sister.

"Awe, my dear twin sister! How are you?" Apollo exclaimed. He released his embrace, finally noticing his sister's expression. He raised his brow at her as if he were asking her what was wrong.

She stared back with a fearful glare in her eyes. Her lips began to tremble with each syllable she spoke. "He knows." She muttered with hardly enough air behind her voice.

Hermes' eyes widened. His olive-toned skin depleted to a pale, ghostly white. Apollo, still in denial, didn't want to accept the fear pouring into his heart. His words began to shake as well. "What in Gaia are you talking about?"

Artemis took her brother's hand, squeezing it tightly. "I'm so sorry. I wish I could help."

A loud voice echoed through the courtyard, rumbling like thunder. "Apollo! Hermes! Come to the throne room at once!"

Chills crept down the three deities' necks. Apollo sighed in acceptance before looking back at Artemis. He nodded his head in sincerity, a sight only ever seen by her and occasionally Hermes. "Thank you for the warning, sister."

"I pray he shows you both mercy." Artemis' eyes glossed over, though she knew better than to show any weakness on Olympus. She knew her father could smell it, prey on it, and punish her for it. Even as fierce a warrior as she was, she was still no match for the God of the Heavens.

Apollo and Hermes both looked back at Artemis as they began their descent down the pathway to the throne room. They walked in silence for what felt like an eternity. The brothers froze for a moment at the towering arched entrance of the marbled palace, taking one last timid breath before walking in.

Entering the throne room, they felt as though they were merely children again; Small, weak, and defenseless. Their father was much larger than them, as well as the other Gods. No one could stop the giant. His white mane nearly touched the top of the vaulted ceilings and matched his long, static-filled beard that was loosely in the shape of a lightning bolt. Hermes and Apollo used to make bets on whether or not this occurred naturally. He wore a purple robe, which was tied off across his waist, highlighting his bulging, boulder-like physique. His muscles looked as if they were carved out of stone. Lightning sparked in his eyes. The brothers reluctantly awaited their father's words as Zeus sat upon his throne, slowly clicking his fingers against the arm of the gold-trimmed chair. "My two dearest sons. I've put so much trust in you over the ages. I've confided in you, fought beside you, and given you the gift of eternal life. And yet you still lie to me. *WHY?*" His voice rumbled with impatience.

In a last-ditch effort, Hermes attempted to do what he was best at: lie and cheat his way out of the situation. "What is it you are referring to, Father?"

Though the God of the Skies could already sense the fear in his son's heart. He could see right through him. He could see all. Thunder boomed throughout the throne room, paving the way for the sharpness of Zeus's tongue. "Don't play stupid with me, boy. I know you've been going down to the mortal realm!"

"And where did you hear this baseless claim?" Apollo, still playing along, placed his hands on his hips as if he were offended by the accusation.

Zeus let out a deep and long maniacal chuckle, which crept right into both his sons' ears and into the deepest, darkest corners of their heads, where only their fears lie. "Baseless, you say? We will see about that." Zeus turned and shouted for yet another one of his children to come forth. "Hephaestus! Fetch me your invention!"

Hephaestus, the God of Invention, though brilliant, was considered the black sheep of the family due to his disfigured face. His disfigurement was the result of his father, Zeus, deeming him too average in appearance to be a god and hurling him off the mountain shortly after his birth. Years later he was eventually accepted on Olympus, but only after his father realized he could use the God's gift of invention for his own gain. He limped in the room, bringing a large, glowing, television-like sphere to Zeus. "I'm so sorry, my brothers; he forced me to…"

Zeus growled thunderously, chucking a golden chalice at Hephaestus's head upon hearing the regret in his least favorite son's voice. In the family of Olympians, weakness was not tolerated. "That's enough out of you, eyesore. Now get back to your workshop!"

Hephaestus shamefully hobbled out of the throne room as Zeus focused his eyes back on Hermes and Apollo. "Now, why don't we see what this contraption can do?" Zeus waved a hand over the orb, showing an image of Apollo burning the man at the bar within the glass ball. "What was it you were saying about baseless claims?"

Apollo looked down in defeat, while Hermes lashed out at him. "I told you he would know!"

Zeus scoffed. "My dear boy, this is just as much your fault." Zeus waved the orb again, and the image rewound back to when Hermes took the man's wallet. "You have all the divine riches you could ever possibly want, yet you still pickpocket trash from those creatures? You just couldn't help yourself, could you?"

"All the riches I could ever want? You keep us all prisoners here! No wonder we want to go to Earth, which is dying, by the way, because you forbade us from going down there!" Hermes attested in one futile and final act of defiance.

Seconds passed like eons as the echo of his words

faded into the chilled Olympus air. Static stiffened the hairs across Hermes's neck, a feeling all too familiar to him. Lightning flickered from his father's hand. A luminously blinding force charged Hermes, piercing him in the chest. Clattering like a hammer against steel, his body was propelled through the air, smacking into a marbled column. Apollo looked back worried, but even the hot-tempered and pompous god knew better than to trifle with his father.

Standing to his feet, Hermes fought for air. As he caught his breath, he began to chuckle, his laughter one of little humor. "Look at you, sulking on your throne because they abandoned you for *Jesus*." He laughed as if it were the last thing he'd ever do. "Could you be any more insecure?"

Apollo's mouth fell to the floor as he anxiously watched his brother's next movements. He wanted to look away, though he couldn't. Hermes was known to have pushed his father's buttons throughout the eons but never to this extent. It was a near death sentence, but Apollo still couldn't help but find himself in agreement with his brother's comments, as would any of the other Gods atop Olympus.

Zeus scoffed at his son's venomous remarks. "Your words are nothing but the desperate cries of vermin moments before slaughter. I should kill you for your disdain—but that would be too merciful—wouldn't it?" Thunder cracked as both brothers looked at each other, bidding farewell. With nothing left to say, the king had made his verdict. "I ruled that fraternizing with mortals was forbidden. Not only did you disobey my orders, but you also lied about it to my face and openly disrespected me in my throne room. For that I can't forgive you, even if you're of my own loins." Zeus raised his hands to the heavens, a rush of rich, dark gray clouds swarmed the two like the smoke of a forest fire; a flurry of lightning soon followed, flickering across their skin, scorching them. The force of the winds swept them up in the air.

"Your punishment will fit the crime. If you love mortals so much, then I banish you to live among them. From now on your godhood will be stripped from you, and you will live and die as mortals!" The two brothers' golden glow faded away as they floated helplessly in the storm surrounding them. Zeus' voice echoed through the thunder. "Now, be gone!"

The storm viciously threw the cursed sons out of the throne room and off Olympus. They flailed their arms throughout the night sky. Their screams choked against the howling winds as they plummeted towards earth. Chilled waves cut against their skin as the brothers crashed into the ocean. Salty from the sea and groaning in pain, they washed up to the shore, coughing up gulps of dirty water, before finally managing to catch their breath.

Apollo exhaled deeply before he turned towards Hermes with a concerned expression he had never truly made before. "I-I feel weak… Where are we?"

Hermes looked across the sands of the beach shining in the dusk and saw a boardwalk riddled with small shops and palm trees scattered about. He squinted, trying to read the signs on the shops, though everything suddenly looked fuzzy. His vision was no longer perfect. He finally managed to make out the name of one of the shops. He blinked profusely as he rubbed his eyes. "From the looks of it, back in Los Angeles. Venice, specifically."

The two stood in silence for a moment, looking out at the waves. Apollo turned back towards his brother, shaking his head. "So you stole his wallet. You really just couldn't help yourself?"

Hermes sighed, pinching the bridge of his nose. "Look, we can sit around forever pointing fingers, but remember, you're the one who charred a man to death."

Apollo scoffed at his brother's accusation, though after a few seconds of contemplation, he decided Hermes might have a point. He conceded a reluctant sigh of acceptance. "I suppose I did let my temper get the best of me… again. But still you have a problem with thievery that needs addressing."

Hermes stood up, offering his brother a hand. "You know I'm the God of Thievery, right?"

"Not anymore." Apollo chuckled and took his hand.

Hermes patted his brother on the back reassuringly. "Don't worry, I have a plan for that."

Apollo gasped sarcastically. "Oh, let me guess, you're going to steal something."

A very familiar smirk started to creep from the corners of Hermes' mouth. "Something like that."

Apollo rolled his eyes, unsurprised. "And what might that be, dear brother?"

Hermes looked up at the sky and back at his partner

in crime. A devilish grin now peeked from ear to ear. "Our father's head."

CHAPTER 2
A DIVINE COUP

STRIPPED OF THEIR godhood and cast down to
Earth, the brothers wandered aimlessly around the
coast of Venice Beach as they struggled to adjust to the
sudden symptoms of mortality. Sunlight soaked their
suits with sweat. Sand stuck to their skin, fastening
into every crevice. The soured stench of seawater
reeked off their tattered and mildewed suits.
Sensations such as perspiration and sunburns were
foreign to the former Gods until now. Hermes
impatiently flicked a bead of sweat from his brow. The
former Messenger of the Gods couldn't tell what was
worse: the sand clumping together in his loafers or his
brother's newfound tone deafness.

Apollo's voice cracked as he attempted his signature
falsetto: "The disgraced Gods, forgotten brothers!" All
that remained of the God of Music was his blind

confidence.

Hermes, unable to bear his brother's piercingly sharp tone much longer, groaned vexingly as he pleaded. "Please, for the love of what Gods are left, stop singing."

Apollo scoffed in disbelief, still unaware of just how talentless he'd become. "Just because I'm not the God of Music anymore doesn't mean I can't still carry a tune." Apollo's voice had become raspy from singing all morning.

"Well, being the God of Music definitely helped you." Hermes walked ahead, hoping a few steps might make Apollo more tolerable. He fidgeted in his loafers, attempting to get the sand out from between his toes. "And besides, I have too much on my mind for a song. I'm trying to figure out how to dethrone the God of all Gods right now." In a fit of frustration, he pulled off his shoe, hurling it to the ground as he lashed out at his brother. "And to make matters worse, I have sand in my shoes!" Hermes's left eye began to twitch.

Apollo chuckled patronizingly as he put his softball-sized bicep around his brother. "Oh, cheer up, brother! At least we've been banished somewhere with a little taste." Apollo nodded his head towards the beach and all its complementary features. Bronzer-coated bodies tanned by the water, strained red bodybuilders wrangled weights at Muscle Beach, and skunk-scented skaters nonchalantly cruised by on their boards. The platinum haired hunk looked right at home amongst them. "Waves, sun, and all the eye candy you could want. It's just like ancient Athens!"

"Ah yes, but now we have to worry about things like plague and famine. What a treat!" Hermes snarled.

Apollo spoke in what he thought was a reassuring tone. "Don't get your loincloth in a twist. We've been down here countless times before. I myself even spent a year as a mortal an eon or so ago. It was a great experience."

Hermes side-eyed his brother coldly. "That doesn't count; you just fucked a king for a year, so you didn't have to do any servant duties."

"Is there any more important duty?" Apollo shrugged, smirking as he fondly thought back on the experience.

Hermes ignored his brother's tasteless quip; he was not in the mood for jokes. He continued to drill into his brother the severity of the situation. "There will be no kings to coddle you this time. We haven't truly been down here as mortals." As he finished his sentence, he stepped on an anthill in the sand. He looked down in defeat at the panicking ants crawling across his foot. "Now we are just ants on a hill waiting to be crushed by humanity's weight."

Apollo cocked an eyebrow up at his brother, chuckling awkwardly. "When did you get so pessimistic?"

"I'd say somewhere in between you burning a man alive and our father disowning us probably did it." Hermes' lifeless eyes remained fixed on the ants.

At that moment, a seagull landed a few feet from the brothers. The bird opened its beak to reveal a refreshingly familiar voice interrupting their bickering.

"Are you two giving up already?" The voice said playfully.

Apollo turned around and looked down at the bird, his face lit up in delight. "Dear sister!" He exclaimed. "Am I glad to see you!" He rushed to hug his twin. He hastily walked towards the bird, which began to shimmer like moonlight painted across a lake. The sparkling grew blindingly bright before revealing the silver-haired Goddess in its wake.

Artemis was disguised as a mortal, and certainly one with style. She wore black jeans, combat boots, and a tattered flannel shirt layered with a timber-hued pleather jacket. The Goddess accessorized with a pair of silver crescent earrings and carried a corduroy fanny pack that seemed to be glowing from the inside. She took off her turquoise-tinted Ray-Bans, shining a crystal-cool grin before embracing her brother, relieved to see he hadn't gotten himself killed yet.

Hermes shuffled over to his siblings, looking melodramatic as ever. Though still scorned, he couldn't help but be curious about his half-sister's arrival. "How'd you manage to sneak off Olympus? I figured Father would have the place under close watch."

Artemis laughed at her brother as she wiped the lens of her glasses against her flannel. "You two think you're the only ones who've come down here against Father's orders? You're just the only ones who've been caught."

Hermes looked at Artemis with a cold and bitter stare. "So did you merely come down here to gloat?"

Apollo dismissively patted Hermes on the back

with faux cheer. "Pardon our half-brother, dear sister. Hermes is a little soured from the whole ordeal of being cast down from the heavens."

Reeking of seawater and despair, Hermes folded his arms as he huffed and puffed in resentment.

Artemis continued. "As much as the Gods love to gloat, I'll admit I come for reasons far more pressing."

Apollo chimed in enthusiastically. "So then to what do we owe the pleasure of this visit?"

Artemis's pale skin glittered in the sunlight as she spoke. "Zeus has gone mad. His spiteful vow against mortals is slowly killing the planet. Without the God's protection of this domain, Gaia will slowly die…"

Hermes, somewhat intrigued, perked up slightly. "So you want to stage a coup against the God of all Gods? Well, easier said than done; I've been trying to solve that puzzle all morning."

"Even with the power of every Olympian combined, we still wouldn't be a match for him." Apollo added.

Artemis giggled, shaking her head. "You dumb boys and your primitive ways." She smirked at her brothers. "Who said anything about fighting?"

"So are you going to tell us or just continue to build anticipation?" Hermes looked annoyed; he hated not knowing things.

Artemis cheekily rolled her eyes at Hermes. "Don't get your loincloth in a twist, brother."

Apollo grinned at Hermes, who scrunched his face in return.

Artemis began to explain her plan. "Thousands of years ago, this island was home to a rare species of flower: nightshade. This flower was rumored to have immense poisonous properties. Of course Gods can't be killed, though a poison like that would have quite the subduing effect on our dear father. If you can find that flower, I can slip it to him while he sleeps. That should knock him out long enough to chop him up and take him to Tartarus."

Hermes scratched his chin, intrigued. "An interesting proposal, but tell me, how does that help us gain our godhood back?"

Artemis spoke nonchalantly. "Oh that? You just need to eat a little of his flesh. A finger for each of you should do the trick."

Hermes and Apollo grimaced at the idea of consuming flesh, let alone their father's.

Apollo shook his head doubtfully. "It'll be hard to get a finger if he turns to smoke and lightning. You know he loves to do that when he's mad."

"Don't fret, brother; he should turn back to his true form once he's unconscious." Artemis reassured her twin brother.

"And where might we find this flower?" Hermes questioned, warming up to the idea.

Artemis clicked her tongue. "It is said to have grown deep in the valleys of this region, only to be seen in the moonlight's glow."

Apollo tilted his head in confusion. "Only to be seen in the moonlight's glow?"

"She means nightfall, simpleton." Hermes sighed.

Apollo rolled his eyes. "So we have to find a flower on a mountain in the dark? Sounds easy enough."

"Easy enough for Gods, but you keep forgetting we don't have our divine powers anymore." Hermes scolded.

Artemis grinned. "Speaking of that, I brought gifts for each of you, courtesy of Hephaestus." Artemis opened the fanny pack around her waist and miraculously pulled out a pair of sneakers and, even more impossibly, an electric guitar. Both items radiated with divine magic. She handed the sneakers to Hermes and the guitar to her twin. "I figured you both would feel bare without your usual trinkets, so I had Hephaestus forge these for you. Of course they have a bit of a modern twist to the originals, just so you don't stand out too much."

Hermes pulled his sand-filled loafers off with haste and laced up the white sneakers decorated with the emblem of a wing stitched into each side. With a click of his heels, the soles began to glow, raising him slightly off the ground. He began to smile. "I must say, it's much more stylish than the winged sandals."

Apollo ran his hands down the neck of the golden V-shaped guitar; its silver strings shimmered in the sun. "This is rather large for a lyre but nonetheless exquisitely crafted. Sister, you never cease to amaze me!"

Hermes clicked his heels again, returning to the ground. He bowed his head, reluctantly conceding to his half-sister. "He's right, we are in your debt, Artemis. How could we ever repay you?"

Artemis patted Hermes on the shoulder. "Why don't you start by getting me that plant?" She began to walk down the beach towards a flock of seagulls. "I'll come back here in a month, so make sure you find it by then. Other than that, just make sure you don't do anything too stupid. Remember, you can die now." The Goddess waved at her brothers.

Hermes and Apollo watched as Artemis disappeared into the flock of seagulls flying away into the sky.

Hermes chuckled in amusement as he nudged his brother. "The Gods love their dramatic exits, don't they?"

"If I had a piece of gold for every time she turned into a bird, I'd be richer than Plutus." Apollo plucked the strings of his guitar, sounding more melodic with each note struck.

Hermes twirled his brown curls, looking puzzled. "Speaking of gold, we should find a way to make some —but how?"

Just then Hermes noticed the crowd surrounding Apollo as he played up and down the neck of his guitar. Beach bums and tourists alike couldn't help but marvel at the passionate flurry of melodies flourishing about the boardwalk. The song ceased gracefully as Apollo looked up to see the crowd cheering for him as they threw loose bills down at his feet. Apollo smirked up at his brother. "Look, brother! They love me!"

Hermes grinned back as if he'd found the answer to their dilemma. "Well, this is going to be easier than I thought."

CHAPTER 3
THE GAMES

IT WAS THE day of the annual Olympic Games back in the golden age of the Gods. The crowd of deities roared throughout the coliseum. Athena had counted the days to this moment. At last she would sit beside the God of the Skies, judging Olympus's finest athletes. The Goddess of Wisdom always appreciated a good contest, though she was more so looking forward to showing off her keen eye for strategy to her father. Even while practicing her drills that morning she'd been so distracted she nearly took Hephaestus's head clean off. Now at last, She sat beside her father's throne, eyes fixed on the ring where Apollo and Ares prepared for their championship bout.

Zeus leaned towards her as the bell rang. "Enjoying yourself, my dear?"

"More than I can say," Athena answered, the glow

in her face betraying her usual composure.

Zeus's smile was faint, measured. "Anything for my little Thena."

Athena momentarily rested her head on her father's shoulder though was alerted by laughing and cheering, looking down to see Apollo standing over the God of War, who was flat on his butt. Athena began to clap, turning to her father. "Well we have a winner, and one in spectacular fashion. Albeit it was rather quick." she was interrupted by the boom of her father's voice echoing down to the ring.

"Why did you stop, boy? Keep fighting.," Zeus's words were ice cold.

Apollo hesitated, lowering his fists.

"Keep fighting." Zeus said, his voice harder, eyes sparking with distant lightning.

The crowd shifted uneasily. Ares wiped the blood from his lip and shook his head.

"Father, the match is over," Athena said, but Zeus didn't look at her.

Apollo glanced up at the throne, saw the storm building in his father's eyes, and turned back to Ares. The next punch landed harder. Then another. Soon the blows came like hail in a tempest, driving Ares to his knees while the crowd fell to a horrified silence.

Athena stared dumbstruck at her father. She'd never seen this side of him before. "Father, that's hardly sportsmanlike, the match is clearly over."

Zeus turned to her, sparks flickered from his stare. "Make no mistake my little Thena, I would do the same to you if you disappointed me."

Athena's breath caught. She searched her father's face for a hint of jest, but the lightning in his eyes told her there was none. Her fingers tightened on the armrest of her throne as she turned back to the ring.

Apollo no longer saw Ares in front of him. With each punch thrown, he channeled his hate for his father. His knuckles cracked against his brother's skull. The thud of Ares' head bouncing off the canvas filled the stadium.

Ares stopped moving, his eyes staring past Apollo into the endless sky above the ring. The crowd sat frozen, their cheers turned to a stunned, collective pity. Athena felt her stomach twist as she wondered whether the Games had been about honor at all — or merely a stage for her father's cruelty.

CHAPTER 4
THE GOD OF MUSIC

THE BROTHERS WALKED down the street through downtown Venice, passing a rainbow of old painted shops all sharing the same tattered brick design. They stopped at a baby blue building, a nightclub with a pink neon sign glowing luminously, that read "Ziggy's." A paper sign dangled below on the window of the club that read "Open mic tonight!"

Hermes nudged his brother excitedly, "This is the place, brother!" Hermes pulled a flier out of his leisure coat and showed it to Apollo.

Apollo rolled his eyes. "I don't understand why I couldn't just keep playing at the beach; you know I love the sun." He was never one to do things on others' terms.

"Yes brother, I'm well aware, but this way you can actually make us money. With your new guitar, they'll be begging us to come back every night!" Hermes persisted.

Apollo shot Hermes a side-eyed stare. "Us? Last time I checked, I'm the one with the guitar, as well as the former God of Music. What is it you're doing?"

Hermes grinned devilishly. "Ah yes, well someone needs to manage you, of course."

"Manage me? Ha! And what makes you think you could manage a musician, let alone Apollo himself?"

Hermes patted his brother on the back in a humbling fashion. "First off, speaking in the third person is quite pompous, a trait you don't need any more of. Secondly, if it weren't for me, you wouldn't have a stringed instrument to begin with!"

"So what exactly would you do as my manager?" Apollo grumbled.

Hermes shined his nails against his coat. "Oh, just the odds and ends, book performances, manage funds, that kind of thing."

Apollo pondered for a moment, grazing his hand on his chin. "I do hate talking numbers… fine," he conceded, "you have yourself a deal, brother. Or should I say, manager!"

Hermes clapped his hands together in a finalizing manner. "Now that that's taken care of, shall we go show these mortals the music of the Gods?"

Apollo sported an arrogant smirk as they walked into the club. "I couldn't agree more!"

The club had more red velvet furnishings than it did lighting, and the stench of marijuana lingered throughout the room. Upon entrance, a slender man with a comb-over and poorly done tie unenthusiastically greeted them while managing to never take his eyes off his pager. "Welcome to Ziggy's. Happy hour is from four to four fifteen pm. Sit wherever you'd like; performances are about to start."

Hermes cleared his throat to get the man's attention. "We're actually here to perform."

The man looked up from his pager and saw Apollo holding his guitar. "Oh well, would you look at that, you are! So what's your stage name? Goldilocks?"

Apollo looked down at the man, offended. "Stage name? Why, I'm Apollo, the God of Music, of course!" He put his arms up in the air, posing in a grandiose fashion.

Hermes pinched his brow and mumbled. "So much for humility…"

The slender, balding man looked up unimpressed. "Uh, that's kind of long. I'm just gonna put Apollo…"

Apollo showed his teeth to the man, hissing angrily, "You will put the God of Music, or so help me, I'll skin you alive!"

The man stepped back, chuckling nervously. "Yeah, okay, sure, man, whatever you want." He unsteadily jotted down Apollo's name onto his clipboard. "Alright, you can go get ready backstage with the other bands. You'll be on in a few." He gestured his head towards the curtain opening to the right of the stage.

The two made their way backstage, watching the band currently performing.

Apollo dramatically tilted his sunglasses down to check out the band, murmuring in distaste. "This is what is considered music now? They just keep playing the same four chords…" He peeled back the curtain leading behind the stage, scoffing at the sight of acoustic guitars and desperation. "Peasants. None of them are a match for me."

Hermes nudged his brother, "Be nice, brother; we don't need a repeat of the Morpheus incident."

Apollo looked annoyed simply from the memory. "Well, maybe if he didn't boast about that damned flute so much, he'd still have his skin."

Hermes patted his brother on the back, trying to calm him down. "Let's try to avoid the subject of skinning, okay? Just focus on putting on a good show. Remember, if you don't then we're homeless."

Just then the band from on stage walked back behind the curtains and up towards the brothers. The frontman waved at Apollo and Hermes. "Hey, man! Sick guitar!"

Apollo refused to look down at the short singer sporting coke bottle glasses and spiked brown hair. "My guitar was forged by the Gods; it's in perfect health. There's nothing "sick" about it."

The frontman looked confused. "Uh, cool dude. Well, I'm Rivers, and this is my band. We just wanted to say good luck! These open mics can be a lot less stressful if we're all friends, right?"

Apollo tuned his guitar, ignoring the entire band. Hermes glared at his brother, though there was no getting through to his ego. He turned to the band, nodding his head politely. "Thank you for the kind words, gentlemen. Best of luck to you as well." Hermes waved them off before quietly reprimanding Apollo. "Would it kill you to at least be cordial? They're fellow musicians, after all."

Apollo took his sunglasses off for the first time upon entering the building, only for a moment to clean them against his turtleneck. "They're not musicians; they're imposters. I mean, what the fuck even is an island in the sun?" He stared bullets back at the band. "If this were the ancient days, their skin would already be off their bodies and fashioned into coats."

Hermes sighed, hanging his head.

Just then the crackling voice on the club's speakers began to announce the next performance. "Tonight we have a newcomer to the amateur scene. Ladies and gentlemen, put your hands together for Apollo—the, uh, God of Music!"

Apollo turned to Hermes, clearly offended once more. "Amateur? The fucking nerve!"

Hermes hissed impatiently. "Dear gods, just get on the stage…" He pushed his brother through the velvet curtains and onto the stage. "Don't fuck this up for us!," he pointed sternly at Apollo before closing the curtains.

Apollo walked out onto the stage, overlooking a few dozen people drinking and chatting. He gripped his guitar, maxing out the potentiometer as he stared down the audience. His glasses tilted slightly down as he leaned into the mic, smirking at the dozen sets of eyes staring up at him. "You're in for quite the treat."

Hermes rolled his eyes, along with most of the other audience members, before Apollo struck a chord on his guitar, blowing the audience's hair back. They began to cheer. The God of Music sang with an angelic tone through a demonic range. The melodies he played seemed to both provoke a sense of nostalgia and yearning for the future. Goosebumps prickled across every soul in the room as he delivered a guitar riff so quickly it would make most players' fingers bleed. He nodded his head in time, enjoying his own music almost as much as his fans. Apollo looked right at home as he glittered under the stage lights. Reaching the guitar solo portion of the song, he leaned back into the crowd, being carried across the room as they chanted his name.

***

All had gone according to Hermes's plan. With his brains and his brother's enchanted guitar, they managed to earn themselves a weekly show at Ziggy's. And with the minuscule payment given to them by the thin, balding club owner, they were just able to afford an apartment. What it lacked in space was made up for in character—or so the brothers would often say defensively. Everything seemed to be looking up, until a loud rumble began to shake within the brothers' guts.

Hermes, in a Venice tourist t-shirt about a size too small, desperately searched through the barren refrigerator in the cramped kitchen of their run-down studio apartment, hoping that if he looked long enough, food would magically appear. He grumbled, his blood sugar lowering for what felt like the first time. "The last time I was hungry, I was an infant. I don't remember it hurting this much…" Hermes slammed the fridge door in defeat.

Apollo, wearing an unbuttoned and unflattering Hawaiian shirt, courtesy of the thrift store down the street, leisurely played his guitar as he lay across the foldout sofa in the center of the apartment. "Have you tried cigarettes? They completely curb the feeling."

Hermes looked at his brother slightly more annoyed than usual. "You do realize that doesn't stop your stomach from eating itself? And please, for the love of the Gods, stop smoking in the apartment!"

Apollo took a deep puff of his cigarette hanging out of his mouth before blowing it out his nostrils. "Sorry, old chap, but it helps the creative juices flow. After all, it is my creativity paying for this place." Apollo took another drag of his cigarette hanging from his lips and grinned smugly. For the first time, his youthful face seemed weathered. He had bags under his eyes and a five o'clock shadow prickling across his face.

Hermes sighed. "Well, we would've been able to afford food if someone didn't throw a fit to be by the beach."

"Once again, my dearest of brothers, creative juices." Apollo continued to play guitar.

A knock at the door caught their attention. The knock was more of a melody, one that was friendly. Hermes walked towards the door, muttering to himself. "I'm guessing answering doors doesn't get the juices flowing?"

Hermes opened the door to a handsome, narrow-faced man in his late twenties, with round glasses and light brown hair down to his shoulders.

The young man greeted Hermes with a warm smile and a casserole in hand. He spoke nervously. "Uh, hi! Uh, I'm Lance. I'm your landlord, I live next door. Sorry to bug you, but I saw you guys moving in earlier, so I figured I'd bring over my famous casserole to welcome you to the building." He smiled softly.

Hermes sniffed the entree, becoming wide-eyed with excitement. "By the Gods, that smells heavenly!" He snatched the casserole from Lance's hands, waving him inside. "Please, please come in! I can't thank you enough." He ripped foil off the dish, grabbing a chunk of casserole and shoving it in his mouth. "I thought we were going to starve!" Bits of casserole flew across the room.

He looked at Hermes, somewhat puzzled by the fact he wasn't using a fork and the almost primal way he was devouring the casserole, but decided to be nice and pretend not to acknowledge it. "Yeah, sure, of course— I'm, uh, glad you—like it." He smiled awkwardly, pausing for a moment. "So, uh, what brings you to Venice?"

Hermes continued to chew yet another large hunk of food. "Well, you see, I'm Hermes, and that's my brother Apollo." Hermes gestured to his brother, still smoking and playing guitar.

Apollo nodded at Lance. "Pleasure."

Hermes continued. "My brother's an aspiring musician, and I'm his manager."

Apollo scoffed. "Aspiring implies I'm not already."

"Oh hush!" Hermes snapped.

Lance looked impressed. His eyes fluttered with intrigue. "Oh wow, that must be exciting! I'd love to come see one of your shows sometime."

Apollo lit another cigarette nonchalantly. "It'd be an honor for you."

Hermes rolled his eyes. "Please, Lance, forgive my brother's grotesquely inflamed ego." He shot a grin at the dashing yet dorky landlord.

Lance chuckled and smiled back, blushing ever so slightly. "Well, I should let you guys get back to your music business. If you guys need anything, I'm just a door down."

Hermes seized the opportunity rather desperately. "Actually, there is one more thing!"

Lance turned back around. "What did you need?"

Hermes tilted his head curiously. "Do you know where I could find nightshade?"

Lance looked puzzled. "Uh, what?"

Hermes reiterated. "Nightshade, you know the flower."

Lance, as he typically did, offered as much help as he could. "I don't know too much about flowers, but we could look it up online if you want."

Hermes cocked an eyebrow up. "I beg your pardon?"

A few moments later, Hermes sat at Lance's computer looking forever changed. "A box that answers any question! Hephaestus himself would marvel at this sight!"

Lance chuckled. "I can't believe you've never heard

of the internet! Where'd you say you're from again?"

Hermes replied somewhat woefully. "Greece, originally."

Lance clicked his tongue. "Must be pretty old-fashioned back there."

Hermes looked off into space for a moment, trying to hide the hate in his eyes. "Oh, you have no idea…"

Lance, noticing Hermes' look of distaste, attempted to change the subject. "That's really cool you and your brother are so close."

Hermes sighed at the thought of Apollo. "I suppose we do go back a way. Trust me, though, it has some drawbacks. The constant arrogance and smoke in my apartment, for starters."

"Your brother reminds me of mine. Both very confident people, hehe. We used to bicker kind of like you guys." Lance laughed, playfully patting Hermes' shoulder.

Hermes tilted his head with intrigue. "And what stopped you two from bickering?"

Lance was now the one who looked woeful. He hung his head regretfully. "He, uh, he died about a year ago. It was a car accident; the tire blew out."

Hermes looked taken back, which was somewhat surprising considering he used to charter the dead to the underworld. Still, the idea of death was starting to seem much more alarming to the former immortal. "My condolences." He said somberly.

Lance became misty-eyed before quickly wiping his tears. "Thanks…" He looked back up, clearing his throat. "It's funny, the bickering is what I miss most.

Like if I could talk to him one last time, I'd probably just end up chewing him out about not checking his tires, heh."

Hermes grinned back at Lance, feeling disarmed by his genuine nature. Perhaps he found value in the young man's perspective, or rather just comfort.

The two gazed at each other for a moment before the website finished loading. Lance, nervous from Hermes' gaze, looked towards the computer screen. "Hey, check it out! I found it!"

Hermes leaned in over Lance's shoulder to look at the screen. Lance blushed as he read. "It says nightshade actually varies in all sorts of species of plants. It also says it's typically used as a poison." Lance looked up at Hermes with a concerned expression. "What did you say you need this for?"

Hermes quickly thought of an excuse. "It's just, uh, for research purposes, a wholesome hobby, of course… Please continue."

Lance nodded before reading on. "It says it's often found in the form of flowers or berries and that it was even spotted near the Hollywood Hills a few centuries ago. Interesting!"

Hermes smiled mischievously. "Yes, very interesting. Who knew it could be found in berries?" He turned towards Lance. "Tell me, Lance, where might the Hollywood Hills be?"

Lance chuckled. "You're kidding, right?"

Hermes looked unamused. "What is so funny?"

"It's literally spelled out for you." Lance pulled up a picture of the Hollywood sign on the monitor. "See?"

***

As night fell, Hermes and Apollo took the opportunity to go to the Hollywood Hills. Apollo walked up the hill overlooking the Hollywood sign fifty yards or so in the distance. Hermes flew a few feet in the air in front of him.

Apollo groaned as he wheezed his way up the steep grassy terrain. "My feet are killing me…"

Hermes snickered as he floated above Apollo. "Such a shame that lyre of yours doesn't possess flight! It makes me wonder which of us Hephaestus favors more!"

Apollo grabbed a stone and attempted to hit Hermes, though he missed rather embarrassingly. "Oh, will you shut up! I was soaring through the clouds in my chariot far before you were even born!"

"Don't get your loincloth in a twist, brother!" He snickered again and looked over towards the Hollywood sign, spotting a cluster of berry bushes glowing red in the moonlight. "I think I've found it!" He exclaimed, flying towards it in an instant.

Apollo scowled at his brother, muttering as he attempted to catch up. "And he calls me the boastful one." He clawed his way up the hill, dripping with sweat and nearly sick. Shaking his fists in triumph, he fell to his knees as he reached the end of his arduous trek. He stood up, still gasping for air. He began to look for his brother; he was surprised not to have heard a sarcastic remark from him by now. Though as the thought crossed his mind, his brother returned to him, spiraling towards his chest. They collided, falling to the ground.

"You pitiful fools. You really didn't think Father would find out what you're up to?" A large, muscled figure dressed in Trojan soldier armor stood a few yards away. A smug grin peeked from the cowl of his helmet as he drew his sword. Lightning flashed behind him menacingly. He spoke to the brothers.

Hermes groaned unconsciously, though Apollo managed to sit up. He looked up at the Trojan towering over him. He scowled, muttering fatefully. "Ares…"

CHAPTER 5
MY APHRODITE!

IT WAS A rare, peaceful afternoon in the courtyard of Olympus, long before the brothers' fall. Hermes and Apollo drifted lazily in the air, passing a bottle of nectar between them and mangling the words of ancient hymns into something far less reverent.

From the forge, Artemis and Hephaestus paused their work to laugh at the antics. Even Athena, poised in her sword drills, let slip a quick snort of amusement.

The brothers were halfway through the chorus of their most scandalous hymn yet when the courtyard doors slammed open. Ares strode in, his jaw clenched, his bronze skin glowing faintly red with rage. The last note of the song died as the siblings turned toward him.

"Hermes!" Ares bellowed, his voice shaking the marble columns. "Show yourself, coward!"

Hermes drifted to the floor and ducked behind a pillar. "Oh Styx… how did he find out?"

Apollo shot him a withering look. "Seriously? As if the rest of us haven't guessed by now."

"Face me!" Ares roared, stomping forward. "You defiled my beloved Aphrodite!"

Hermes peeked out from the column with a lazy grin. "Well, I wouldn't put it like that. If anything… she started it."

Ares lunged, his spear hand raised — but Apollo caught him by the throat mid-charge, shoving him back so hard he stumbled and hit the marble floor with a clang.

"Some God of War you are," Apollo said, smirking.

For a heartbeat, the courtyard was silent. Then Artemis snorted. Hephaestus started to chuckle. Even Athena hid a smile behind her blade.

Ares flushed crimson to the tips of his ears and stormed away, the sibling's laughter following him out of the courtyard.

CHAPTER 6
THE FORGOTTEN SON

ARTEMIS WALKED THROUGH the marbled courtyard of Mount Olympus. She spotted Athena practicing her swordplay. Athena wore a golden chest-piece and matching Trojan helmet that twinkled against her bronzed-skin. The Goddess of Wisdom nodded in greeting, cool and calculated as always. "Artemis," she said.

Artemis nodded back. The two Goddesses shared a quiet respect. They were often the calmest of the siblings, level-headed in a sea of storms. "Athena," Artemis returned.

Athena continued swinging her sword as she spoke. "The month is nearly over."

"I'm aware." Artemis replied, her expression tight.

Athena's tone dropped, careful and measured. "Do you think the month's end will be fruitful?"

Artemis exhaled, unsure of an answer even though it was the only thing that had been on her mind. "One can only hope." Her gaze drifted across the courtyard to the empty forge of Hephaestus. "Have you seen Hephaestus around?"

Athena tapped the tip of her sword against her chin thoughtfully, only for her face to darken. "Come to think of it, I haven't seen him in the last day or so…"

Artemis stared at the empty forge, dread sinking into her heart. She turned to her sister, unable to hide the look of worry upon her face. "Do you think—"

A voice thundered through the sky, interrupting her. "Artemis! Come to my chamber at once!"

She paled, her silver hair suddenly ghostly against her skin. Athena placed a hand on her shoulder.

Artemis treaded nervously across the courtyard and through the large archway into Zeus's throne room. She stood before an empty throne with a storm cloud flickering with white hot lightning above it. She looked up at the cloud, hiding her shaky hands behind her back. "You called me, Father?"

Thunder rumbled. Zeus's voice boomed from the storm. "My sweet Artemis. You've always been one of my favorite children. When your brothers betrayed me, I took comfort knowing I still had your loyalty."

Artemis replied with haste. "And you still do, Father."

Thunder erupted yet again, echoing up to the vaulted ceilings. "Artemis… I see everything."

Footsteps crept behind Artemis. She turned to see Hephaestus enter the chamber. His hands had been cut off and his eyes torn from their sockets. He stood expressionless, now a shadow of the God he once was.

Tears welled in Artemis' eyes. "No…" He never would've made those items for Hermes and Apollo if she hadn't asked him to.

The room shook with laughter and lightning. "Let's see him forge something for you now." Zeus's thunder rolled again, cruel, and self-satisfied.

Artemis began to shake with rage; her father had gone too far this time. Hephaestus was one of her closest friends atop the mountain. She drew her bow, firing off a silver arrow at the storm, only to be struck down by a bolt of lightning. She glared daggers up at the flickering clouds.

Zeus continued, ignoring his daughter's fit of anger. "Of course I had him forge one more thing for me before I delivered his punishment."

From above, a metal cage descended on thick chains, landing with a heavy clang before her. Zeus looked down at Artemis spitefully, his voice devoid of any affection he once had for his daughter. "Now, get in the cage."

***

While the Gods on Olympus faced their father's wrath, Hermes and Apollo were left to deal with the runt of the litter back in Los Angeles.

Apollo stood off against Ares. The mythical Trojan now towered over his once larger-than-life brother. The God of War was always known to be one of the more insecure Gods despite his intimidating presence and deadly reputation. "I want you to know that I was the one who told Father of your excursions down to the mortal realm." He grinned menacingly. "Now look, the golden child, father's favorite son, is disowned. Ha!"

Apollo scowled for a moment before beginning to smirk. "I suppose that makes you his favorite son now, of course only by default though."

"Father just finally realized who is actually loyal to him." Ares bared his teeth, snarling at Apollo.

Apollo let out an over-the-top laugh. "You mean who would spy for him? Does your daddy's approval really mean that much to you?"

"You don't get it. You've had everything handed to you. You've always been loved. I had to earn it! And even then I was still second to you! What made you so much better? I mean, I'm the only legitimate son on Olympus, for the Gods' sake!" Ares snapped at his older brother, his tone carrying eons of jealousy behind it.

Apollo shrugged, "Well, it's not my fault I was better than you at everything."

"Oh, I'm going to enjoy killing you. Even as a frail mortal."

Apollo stood proud, knowing he at least got under his brother's skin one last time. "Only way you ever could." He fired back.

"So cocky for a dead man. I'm almost impressed." Ares chuckled.

The Hollywood sign glowed beside them, acting as a spotlight for the showdown to come. Words had ceased, leaving only the sound of the sign's generators humming off in the distance. Apollo stared down Ares like a cowboy at high noon, looking as though he might actually pose a problem for the God. Ares removed his helmet, casting it to the ground as horns erupted from his head. His body contorted to the shape of a bull, revving its legs back, steaming from its nostrils. Apollo took one look at the bull before making a break for it, running away as fast as he could. The beast stomped its hooves in frustration before chasing after him.

Huffing and puffing, Apollo was nearly at the Hollywood sign. "Shit—shit—shit," he muttered frantically as he found himself stuck in front of a chain-link fence blocking off the generator bank powering the sign. He tried to think of something to do—anything to do. Though he couldn't think with the loud buzzing of electricity surging through the generators. He looked back at his horned brother catapulting towards him, now only a few seconds away. It was then that an idea so outlandish it just might work crept into Apollo's head. "I have to—time this—just—right..." he said to himself in between wheezes.

The divine creature charged at him ferociously, though at the last second Apollo dove aside, tumbling into the concrete. Unable to stop in time, Ares crashed into the generators. His body jolted uncontrollably as the current of power flowed through him.

Apollo looked on in hopes he had subdued his brother. "Please be out..." He winced.

Ares rose from the wreckage, smoking and furious.

He turned back to his God form, brushing the sparking cluster of wires from his shoulder. His face twisted with rage as he lunged at Apollo, grabbing him by his throat. "Enough games," he said seething as he began to pummel Apollo, his fists crashing down on his skull with a savage force only willed through hate.

Hermes stirred awake nearby. His vision swam for a moment, though it cleared just in time to see his brother being beaten within an inch of his life. "Brother!" Hermes cried out. He looked around for anything that could help him. His gaze shot to the sparking wires behind Ares. Wings on his sneakers sparkled as he launched himself towards Ares.

Ares, still mid-rant, failed to notice Hermes coming. "Who's the better boxer now? Huh?" Apollo's face was now welted and red with blood, though he was still breathing. Ares cocked his fist back in finality. Though before he could deliver the final blow, Hermes slammed feet first into Ares, hurling him back into the live wires. An arc flashed violently, knocking the brothers back. The Hollywood sign flickered before going dark. They looked back to see the God of War lying in the flickering debris, singed and lifeless.

As Hermes helped him up, Apollo looked up at him, surprised by his brother's actions. "You saved me. You could've made a break for it. But you risked your life to save me. Why?"

Hermes looked down at Ares, disappointed. "I suppose that's what family is supposed to do for each other." He turned to Apollo with a smile, though his eyes quickly widened. "Almost forgot!" He darted towards the glowing bush, snapped off a handful of shimmering berries, and stuffed them into his pocket. Beginning to float off the ground, he turned and held a hand out towards Apollo. "Come on, I'll give you a lift home."

The brothers soared through the night sky, looking down at the vibrant city lights below. The Hollywood sign began to flicker back on momentarily before shutting off again, smoke billowing from each letter.

CHAPTER 7
A CHARIOT FOR A GOD

AFTER THEIR BATTLE with Ares, the brothers spent the next morning learning what it meant to heal as mortals do. The pain was excruciating, even with Lance's aid. Apollo and Hermes sat on the couch of their apartment groaning from the plethora of contusions and abrasions they endured courtesy of their younger brother. Lance knelt next to them, holding a tray of soup and two bags of frozen peas.

Lance handed the brothers the frozen peas. "You guys really have to look both ways; LA traffic is no joke."

Given his concussed state, it was a miracle Hermes was able to think of a reasonable excuse for their condition when he knocked on Lance's door at four in the morning, asking for help. Hermes groaned. "Yes, ugh, I suppose we do…"

Lance tilted his head sympathetically. "I'm just sorry you guys got so banged up." He gently rubbed Hermes's face, looking at the purple swelling across it.

Apollo grumbled, wincing as he scowled, bitter of his condition. Other than by his father, it was the first time he'd been defeated in battle or injured for that matter, and the fact it was by Ares of all Gods ate away at him. He festered on the sofa, wearing his sunglasses to cover up a pair of black eyes as well as his shame.

Lance looked at Apollo with a concerned look. "Are you guys going to cancel the show tonight?"

With everything that had happened the night before, Apollo had forgotten about his show entirely. "Thanatos, take me now." He looked up and sighed before wincing in pain again.

***

To both Hermes and Lance's surprise, Apollo played his best show yet at Ziggy's that evening. Apollo stood on stage holding his guitar in the air as the crowd chanted his name. Hermes waited behind the stage as Apollo soaked up the limelight. The platinum-haired wonder bowed boastfully. "You're welcome! You're all welcome! Goodnight!" He waved at his fans before exiting through the dingy velvet curtains leading backstage.

Hermes clapped his hands as his brother approached him. "I'll admit, brother, I'm impressed. I'm not even sure how you pulled that off. I can hardly stand."

Apollo spoke quickly. "I know, right? Honestly, I amaze myself! Perhaps I still have some divine blood flowing through me after all!" He was noticeably jittery. He took off his sunglasses to reveal eyes that were bloodshot with pinpoint pupils.

Hermes, noticing his brother's odd behavior, couldn't help but ask, "Is everything alright, brother?"

Apollo reached into his coat, pulling out a bag of cocaine. He proceeded to open the bag and stick his nose in, inhaling one deep whiff. He looked back up at Hermes while wiping the coke into his teeth. "What? Me? Of course! I'm not just alright, I am thriving, brother!"

Hermes looked at Apollo, unsurprised. "Well, I guess that explains your miraculous recovery…" Hermes sighed. "Look, I love cocaine just as much as the next person, but right now we need to stay focused."

Apollo rolled his eyes. "Oh, brother, would you please lighten up? We already beat Ares, for the Gods' sake!"

As usual, Hermes found himself yet again having to be the voice of reason amongst the two. He spoke sternly, scolding his older brother. "I think you're forgetting that it was sheer luck and that he's still very much alive."

Apollo fiddled with the bag of cocaine as he responded, "Well, if he comes back, now I have something to give me an edge." He sniffed another bump off the back of his hand and grinned. Flakes of coke were sprinkled across his teeth.

Hermes pinched his brow. "Look, I'm in too much pain to deal with this right now. I'm going home to lie down. At least try not to kill yourself while I'm gone..." Hermes turned and walked away.

Apollo, unbothered by his brother storming out, snorted more cocaine and yelled at Hermes as he left. "Your loss, brother!"

Just then an older gentleman in a suit approached Apollo. He was eager though professional and had the swiftness of a vulture about him. "Excuse me, are you the artist known as Apollo?"

Apollo turned around, wiping his gums with his finger. "That depends. Who would like to know?"

"I'm an executive with Sony Records." The man said confidently as he put out his hand to shake Apollo's, though it was sorely rejected.

"Ah yes, in that case, the pleasure is all yours. Tis I, the great Apollo." Apollo nodded to the man in a flippant greeting.

The executive asked curiously. "You don't have a manager, do you?"

"My manager is predisposed at the moment. Tell me, what is it you desire?" Apollo questioned the executive, stepping towards him skeptically.

The man was now getting nervous as he looked up at the wall of muscle standing over him. He dropped his professional facade slightly. "Well, Sony thinks you have a unique sound and aesthetic that, if nurtured right, could make you a household name."

Apollo's nose scrunched up in annoyance, "Nurtured? As if I'm an infant of some kind?"

The man cleared his throat, a cold sweat fell from his brow. "Sony is just concerned with you reaching your true potential. You know, albums, tours, MTV. That could all be yours if you sign with Sony Records."

Apollo pondered the proposal for a moment, looking up at the ceiling as he scratched his chin before muttering, "I suppose that would be amusing..." He looked back at the Sony executive, smiling ear to ear. "Say no more! Where do I sign?"

The man pulled out a contract and pen, handing it to Apollo. Apollo hastily jotted down his autograph.

The executive was already thinking of ways to spend the bonus he'd receive from signing the artist. He smiled thinking about the amount of sex workers and drugs he could buy with it. "Congratulations, Apollo, welcome to Sony Records." The man shook Apollo's hand. "Oh, and as for your compensation." The man reached in his coat, pulling out a check. "I trust this will be a fair initial investment. Don't worry, after you start touring, those checks are going to get bigger." He handed the check to Apollo, who stared bug-eyed at the amount of zeros on the crisp piece of paper.

***

It was the next morning when Hermes found out about his brother's good news, which, in typical fashion, became Hermes's misfortune. He was standing angrily with his arms folded, in a bathrobe in front of the apartment building parking lot. Apollo leaned proudly against a brand-new red convertible Porsche.

Hermes huffed and puffed. "You bought a sports car? With what money?"

Apollo looked at the car proudly. "From the record label."

Hermes looked offended. "The record label? Don't you think that's something you would involve your manager in?"

Apollo brushed him off, perhaps somewhat bitter about his storming out after his show. "Sorry, you were sleeping."

Hermes still looked as if he was trying to wrap his head around the situation. "Did this all happen last night?"

Apollo lit a cigarette and shrugged. "The music business moves fast, baby." Taking a drag of his cigarette, he winked at Hermes.

Hermes let out a frustrated sigh as he questioned his brother. "How much money did the record label give you?"

Apollo grinned. "Sixty thousand dollars. Of course I thought I deserved more."

Hermes raised an eyebrow nervously. "And how much was that car?"

Apollo cleared his throat. "Just about sixty thousand…"

Hermes pulled his curly brown hair nearly out of his scalp. "So you spent all our money on a car?"

Apollo smiled, attempting to reassure Hermes. "Not just any car, a Porsche." He pridefully slapped the hood of the car.

Hermes now had a vein bulging from his forehead from the stress of the situation. "That doesn't make it any better."

Apollo rolled his eyes. "Don't get your loincloth in a twist, brother; we'll make more from the shows at Ziggy's."

"We can't afford to wait till next Friday's show. I've been rationing Lance's casserole for nearly a week." Hermes's stomach rumbled, he placed a hand on it.

"I think I have just the thing that can help with it." Apollo, now back in his car, revved the engine of his Porsche. He shouted over the engine's roar. "See? Now you can't even hear your stomach! You're welcome!" Apollo grinned at Hermes, who looked as stern as a parent waiting up for their teenager.

Hermes rolled his eyes. "Why don't you at least make yourself useful and drive me down to Ziggy's? Maybe the manager will allow an impromptu performance, so we don't go hungry." Hermes got in the car, instantly perking up. "My, my, this is quite comfortable. Aesthetically pleasing as well."

Apollo grinned, "Wait till you feel this." He revved the engine, going well over ninety miles per hour.

Hermes chuckled. "By the Gods, Hephaestus would relieve himself over this!" The two sped down the highway by the beach towards Ziggy's.

***

Unfortunately, Ziggy's fruitfulness would soon turn barren… Hermes pleaded with the club manager.

"What do you mean we can't play here anymore?"

The manager seemed unbothered, still fixed on his pager. "Sorry, guys, but this place is for amateur performers. Now that your brother signed with a record label, we can't afford to split club profits with them. It's nothing personal; you're just too expensive."

Hermes cried out desperately. "Too expensive?"

The manager sighed before turning away. "Sorry, H, it's just business."

Hermes glared at Apollo, "I hope your little car was worth it…"

"Considering I've already had intercourse about 15 times in it, I'd say so." Apollo rebutted arrogantly, refusing to take the situation seriously.

Hermes, nearing his boiling point, ignored Apollo as he stormed past him out of Ziggy's.

"Oh, come on, don't give me the silent treatment!" Apollo sighed as he followed his brother.

Hermes turned sharply around, "As a matter of fact I am, because you have absolutely ruined everything, as usual!" Hermes pointed aggressively, shaking with anger at the pompous rock star. "All of our hard work, down the drain, and you couldn't care less!" He got back inside the Porsche, slamming the door, burying his face into his hands as he sat in silence.

Apollo rolled his eyes as he walked to the passenger-side door, tapping on the glass, pleading with his sulking brother, "Oh, so you're going to pout now?"

Hermes locked the door, forcing his brother to wait outside the Porsche while he stewed. He folded his arms as he stared down at the leather dashboard riddled with white powder. After a few deep breaths and time to think, he finally unlocked the car.

Apollo sat hesitantly in the driver's seat beside him. He paused for a moment. "Did you want to drive?"

He took a deep breath, looking at the coke on the dash again. "No, I'm done pouting. I know how I can make more money."

Apollo looked unamused. "Well, spit it out."

Hermes looked up at his brother. "Who do you buy your cocaine from?"

Apollo began to reach for his bag in his coat. "Oh, I already have some with me if you'd care for a bump."

Hermes sighed. "No, you imbecile, I want to sell it."

CHAPTER 8
DEATH AT THE ORPHEUM

WEEKS WENT BY as the former God of Commerce
and Thievery began what Los Angeles would call one
of the greatest drug epidemics of the century. It wasn't
his first choice, but he figured it was between selling
cocaine and shoplifting, and since his sticky fingers got
him into this mess, he opted for the latter. Not to
mention cocaine's profit margins were significantly
higher. Upon visiting Apollo's original dealer, he was
surprised to find convincing the dealer to give up a
chunk of his profits was easier than expected, due to
him being quite the Apollo fan. Hermes managed to
convince him to make him a middleman for the
operation. He would pick up the shipment, deliver it
with inexplicable haste, and receive about forty percent
in return. *Simple enough, and quite lucrative,* he thought.

Hermes, carrying a satchel at his side, soared across

the skies of Los Angeles, pushed through the clouds by his white wing-engraved sneakers. Giggling like a child, he performed a corkscrew maneuver before landing on top of a building downtown.

Hermes sighed refreshingly; he seemed much more relaxed since his new job had taken off. "Nothing like a good flight to clear my head!"

He walked down the fire escape and into the side alleyway of the building. He casually leaned against the wall of the alleyway and checked his Rolex.

A man with a mustache walked up next to him and leaned against the wall inconspicuously. He spoke without turning towards Hermes. "You got the goods?"

Hermes gave a long dramatic pause before replying, performatively checking if anyone was around. He loved the clandestine theatrics of a drug deal. "That depends, 'stache; you got the cash?"

The man reached into his pocket, subtly handing Hermes an envelope. Hermes reciprocated it with a plastic bag of cocaine from inside his satchel. Hermes put the envelope into his satchel. "Pleasure doing business with you," he spoke as he gave a departing nod to the man. Hermes walked away until he was far enough to fly without anyone seeing him. As he flew through the sky, he heard a buzzing come from inside his bag. He opened it, grabbed his brick phone out, and answered it. "Hello, brother… I'm finishing up now… Yes, I'll be back in time for your show tonight. Yes, I remember where: the Orpheum Theater. Alright, see you then."

Hermes put the phone back in his satchel and proceeded to do a few more corkscrews through the sky before flying off, right over the Hollywood sign.

***

A hundred feet below, a city electrician was driving up to the back of the Hollywood sign. He talked on the radio in his truck. "Checking on the power outage at the sign now, over."

The electrician got out of his service truck and walked over to the still smoking and crushed generators. "What the hell happened here?" He said in awe to himself as a large shadow fell over him. He turned around to see Ares staring down at him, still covered in fried wiring. The man stuttered timidly at the god. "Can—can I help you?"

Ares grabbed the electrician and ripped off his head. He dropped the body and held the head as he scowled into its lifeless eyes. "Vengeance will be mine." He proclaimed, seething with rage, before dropping the head and vanishing away in a mist of blood-colored flames.

***

Later that evening, Hermes walked into the Orpheum, one of LA's oldest and most prestigious theaters. Apollo was on stage in the middle of a guitar solo. Hermes walked to the back of the crowd of people cheering his brother. Hermes looked impressed, proud of his brother's accomplishment. "Quite the turnout." Hermes continued to scan the room aimlessly until he noticed a familiar face, his customer from earlier in the alleyway. *Stache? Huh, it's a small world*, he thought to himself. Hermes watched curiously as the man with the mustache inconspicuously took a bump of coke as he rocked back and forth, dancing with a woman. Hermes began to smile as he considered this evidence of a job well done. Soon after though, the man frantically clutched his chest, dropping to the ground.

The woman began to panic as she desperately tried to jostle him awake. "Henry! Henry! Wake up! Henry, please!" The woman screamed.

Hermes' eyes widened as he looked on in horror. "No…" he muttered woefully.

Mascara ran down the woman's face as she desperately looked out into the crowd for aid. "He's not breathing! Someone help!"

The crowd soon diverted their attention to the unresponsive man on the ground and away from Apollo. Apollo stopped playing, looking annoyed at the crowd. The more heads that turned away from him, the angrier he got. He yelled at the crowd now fixated on the overdosing man. "How dare you all turn your back on the God of Music! Forget that weakling!" The crowd began to boo Apollo in response. "You peasants dare boo Apollo? You should all be worshipping the ground I walk on!" The crowd began to pelt their drinks at him. Apollo lashed back in response, wiping beer from his face. "I'll skin you all alive! Bow before your God!" That was about the time security came and grabbed Apollo, dragging him off stage as he unyieldingly and aggressively squirmed and shouted back at the audience. "Bow or be skinned!" His words echoed down the hall, fading into the crowd's boos.

Hermes, still in a trance, stared at the woman sobbing as she held the man's lifeless body. He was jolted back to reality by his brother's shouting. He looked over at Apollo now being taken out the front doors of the theater. "For the love of the Gods, brother!" Hermes called for his brother in a chastising tone. He looked back again at the woman shamefully and proceeded to follow after his brother.

***

As he flew back to the apartment from the show, Hermes was still stuck in a trance. He couldn't stop thinking of that poor mustached man and the woman with him. *Did he die? Was it my fault?* He thought to himself as he entered the apartment to see Apollo standing there, furious.

Apollo paced back and forth. "Did you see that? That man dying made a mockery of my performance!"

Hermes looked pale as a ghost. "You—you really think he died?"

"Does it matter? Either way, it ruined my show!" Apollo scoffed.

Hermes' sad demeanor quickly shifted to one of bewildered anger. "How could you be so selfish? A man died."

"And that concerns me how?" Apollo rolled his

eyes.

Hermes' eyes turned glossy. "He had a life, people who cared about him! Can't you think about anyone but yourself?"

Apollo looked at Hermes, annoyed by his brother's emotions, though he also seemed confused by his brother's change of heart. "What's got you all hot and bothered? It's not like we knew him or anything."

"It doesn't matter! Not everything has to be about you! A man was hurt; show some respect!" Hermes shouted.

Apollo, still not understanding or caring, continued to argue. "Yes, a man of mortal blood. Disposable like the rest of them."

Hermes got in his brother's face. "Life is precious, brother, immortal or not. And last time I checked, you're one of them too."

"You're beginning to sound like that old kook Prometheus." Apollo laughed.

"And you sound like the one who imprisoned him." Hermes snapped back.

Apollo clenched his teeth. "I am nothing like Father…"

"I wouldn't be so sure about that, brother." Hermes stormed out of the apartment, fuming over his brother's words.

The door slammed behind Apollo as he searched around his pocket, pulling out a pack of cigarettes. He opened it to see it was empty and proceeded to kick the guitar amp down by his foot. "Shit!"

Hermes wiped tears from his eyes as he paced

down the apartment building's hallway. The guilt was consuming him now. He needed to tell someone. Before he knew it, he was knocking on the front door of Lance's place.

***

An hour or so later, Hermes and Lance lay in bed as a swirl of blankets hardly covered them. They stared at the ceiling as Lance ran his finger in a circle around Hermes' chest. Lance questioned his lover sympathetically. "So you want to talk about it yet or fool around some more?"

Hermes sighed. "I've been selling cocaine to help pay for rent."

Lance bent his brow in concern. "You know if you needed money, I could loan you some. You don't have to sell coke."

Hermes sighed, shaking his head. "Oh please no, you've already done enough for me."

Lance leaned closer. "So what is it then?"

Hermes looked troubled as he ran his hand through Lance's dirty-blond hair. "When I was at Apollo's show, I saw one of my customers. A gentleman with a mustache. He was with a woman, and... he overdosed in front of everyone, right after he took a bump of the cocaine I sold him."

Lance put his hand over Hermes' hand. "That's fucked up..."

Hermes started to get teary-eyed. "I don't know if he's dead or not. All I know is that whatever happens to him is my fault. It's strange; I feel so guilty. All I can think about is the look on his date's face."

Lance smiled softly and hopefully at the guilt-ridden Hermes, seeing a silver lining that the new mortal hadn't. Lance explained. "That's called empathy, babe. It's a little concerning that this is the first time you're feeling it, but better late than never, I guess."

Hermes looked down, embarrassed.

Lance put a hand on Hermes's cheek. "Look, what you did was really shitty; you should feel bad, but it doesn't mean you're a shitty person. It's never too late to change, babe. The cool part about life is that you can make as many mistakes as you want. As long as you try to learn from them, I think it'll be okay."

Hermes looked at Lance and began to smile hopefully. Lance smiled back.

"You're a good man, Lance. I aspire to be more like you." Hermes gently stroked his lover's chin with his thumb.

Lance blushed. "Heh, well, I wouldn't go that far, but thanks, you're really sweet."

The two kissed passionately, embracing each other as they fell back into the endless swirl of sheets.

***

As Hermes confided in Lance, Apollo had gone out to buy a pack of cigarettes and presumably brood.

Apollo lit a cigarette as he walked out of the gas station. He took a deep inhale and blew a cloud of smoke off into the night sky. He let out a heavy sigh of relief. "Ahh, thank the gods for cigarettes."

He was heading towards his car when he heard some people shouting behind him. He turned to see a group of men in their early twenties hanging out in the parking lot by their pickup trucks.

One of the young men called out to the rest of his friends. "See, it's him! I told you guys!"

His friend excitedly tapped him on the shoulder. "Holy shit, you're right!"

Apollo smiled smugly, approaching the group of young men all murmuring to each other. "Suppose I have time for some fans." Apollo said to himself.

A third member of the group of young men gestured towards Apollo. "You're that Apollo guy, right?"

Apollo began to greet them in his typical grand fashion, putting his arms out as if he were posing. "Indeed, gentlemen, tis I! Apollo! The God of Mus—"

Just then one of the young men sprung up and delivered a right hook to Apollo's jaw, knocking him to the pavement. "What's wrong? I thought you were gonna skin us all alive? Right?"

The other guys joined in, kicking Apollo in the side as he lay curled in a fetal position. Another chimed in, mocking the disgraced star. "Who's bowing now, bitch?"

The young men ceased their attack, staring down at a bloody and groaning Apollo. "Fucking prick..." One of the young men said as they spat on him before they all got back in their trucks and sped off.

Apollo rolled on the cold concrete as he groaned in pain.

***

The next morning, as Hermes came back to the apartment, he was surprised to see that his dear brother had a sudden change of heart. Apollo sat on the couch with a cigarette in his mouth and a bag of frozen peas, nursing his fresh black eye. Hermes eyed him up and down. "And what happened to you?"

Apollo inhaled his cigarette, ignoring his brother's question. He pulled out an envelope from his coat and handed it to Hermes.

Hermes looked at the piece of paper that seemed to be some kind of invoice. "What's this?"

Apollo exhaled a puff of smoke. He looked uncharacteristically embarrassed, almost timid. "Look outside."

Hermes walked over to the window. He noticed that the Porsche wasn't in its parking spot. He turned to Apollo with a bewildered expression. "You sold it?"

Apollo tried to smile, though he winced in pain. "Now you don't have to sell cocaine anymore."

Hermes' brow softened from his brother's actions. He was at a loss for words. "Brother, I.."

Apollo interrupted as he stared down at the floor. "I don't want to be like Father. Everyone's turned against him. I don't want everyone to turn against me. Especially you."

Hermes put a hand on Apollo's shoulder. "It's never

too late to change, brother. You just have to try." He smiled reassuringly at Apollo. "And don't worry, you're stuck with me."

Apollo managed to finally muster a smile onto his swollen and bruised face.

***

Meanwhile, on Mount Olympus, Artemis watched closely from her cage as the storm in the throne room subsided to a dull grey cloud above the throne and into a large, muscle-bound man with a long white mane. *Finally, he's asleep. Now to get out of here ...* Artemis thought to herself excitedly.

Artemis attempted to turn into a raven but could only grow a beak. She quickly turned her face back and began to pant in exhaustion. "Shit... I can't transform. Hephaestus must have divine-proofed the cage." She hung her head as she slumped against the cage. As she began to accept her fate, she remembered something. Something her father said—or rather didn't say. She thought to herself for a moment, *If Apollo and Hermes were dead, father wouldn't be able to stop himself from boasting about it, yet he didn't mention them at all when we spoke. There's still hope, I just need to stick to the plan ...* She looked back at Zeus again, making sure he was still asleep, then whistled quietly. Shortly after, a raven flew into the throne room, landing on her cage. She whispered to the raven. "Go west and find Hermes and Apollo. They'll give you a flower; bring it to me." The raven nodded before flying off. Artemis looked back at

Zeus and muttered to herself. "Please have the nightshade…"

CHAPTER 9
THE BURNING CITY

HERMES AND HIS father stood atop the hill overlooking the burning city. Lightning rained from the heavens, scorching every soul in its path.

Below them, an elderly couple hurried away from the flames. They never looked back despite the thousands of screams rising like a storm behind them. After all, their God told them not to. Tears ran down their soot-stained cheeks; each new crack of lightning made them flinch, squeezing each other's hand tighter.

Zeus stood with his hands on his hips, the firelight gleaming off his silver beard. A faint smile tugged at his lips as he stared proudly at a job well done. He slapped a heavy hand on Hermes' shoulder, "This is what they earn for worshiping false Gods. No respect. No decency. After all I've done for them… they deserve the fire."

Hermes had seen death before — in wars, in plagues — but never like this. The air reeked of smoke and burnt flesh. The cries from below rose above his father's voice, ragged and desperate. He wondered if any victory could be worth such a sound.

Zeus's smile faded upon noticing the doubt across his youngest son's face. He seized Hermes by the collar and dragged him a step closer, eyes sparking with storm-light. "Do not mourn these vermin. Their lives mean nothing. Without me, they would not exist. Without me, you would not exist. The only thing you share with them is that you both serve me." Zeus threw him to the ground.

Hermes' gaze lingered on the old pair, huddled together, whispering thanks to the Gods for their lives. Their faces were wet with both rain and tears.

Zeus's grin was almost playful as he tilted his head towards them. "Even those two… as loyal as they are —"

A bolt split the night, and the hilltop where they stood erupted in white light. When Hermes' vision cleared, there was nothing left of them but ash drifting in the wind.

"- they never really mattered."

Hermes jolted awake, breath hitching, the sheets damp against his skin.

Lance stirred, blinking sleepily and brushing a hand across Hermes's cheek. "Hey… you okay?"

Hermes swallowed hard. "Yeah. Just a dream."

Lance pressed a soft kiss to his temple and settled back down. "I'm here. Wake me if you need me, babe."

Hermes lay staring at the ceiling, his pulse still hammering. The cries from the burning city lingered in his ears, refusing to fade.

CHAPTER 10
CALM BEFORE THE STORM

THE NEXT DAY Apollo awoke to a raven pecking at their living room window. He skipped down the hall, eagerly knocking on Lance's door.

Lance opened the door, wearing a fuzzy robe and holding a mug of coffee larger than his fist. He spoke softly, still half asleep. "Hey Apollo, you're up early."

"Ah yes, what an astute eye you have Lance. Listen, could you grab Hermes for me? It's rather important." Apollo posted his arm casually against the door frame.

Lance gestured to the door behind him. "He's in the shower but I can give him a message when he gets out if you want."

"Ah yes, well just tell him there's a— raven pecking at our window…" Apollo stammered.

Lance sipped his coffee and nodded his head. "Right on, I'll uh be sure to let him know. You know you didn't strike me as the bird watching type."

Apollo paused for a moment before clicking his tongue. "Yes, well um one can never have too many hobbies I suppose... Anyway, I better get going. Farewell Lance!"

"Alright, later man. Have a good day." Lance waved at Apollo as he walked down the hall.

***

Twenty minutes or so later, Hermes sat in front of the coffee table packing nightshade into a small glass jar, while his brother played with the raven at the windowsill. He stood up from the sofa, sealing the jar.

"You know that thing will probably give you the bird flu, right?" Hermes said, handing the jar to Apollo.

Apollo shrugged as he took the jar. "I'm sure I've had worse hangovers." Apollo handed the jar to the raven, who bit onto the cap with its beak.

Hermes scolded his brother. "You're forgetting again that you can die now."

Apollo petted the raven with his finger. The bird nodded before flying away. Apollo looked out hopefully at the winged messenger fading in the skyline. "Not for much longer."

A troubled expression fell across Hermes's face. "I suppose so."

Apollo turned towards his brother. "So now what?"

"Now we wait," Hermes replied, sitting back on the sofa.

Apollo threw his head back and groaned. "Oh, by the Gods, again?"

And so the brothers eagerly waited for Artemis to get back to them. Hoping that the other Gods, as well as their plan, stayed intact.

***

Back on Mount Olympus, the skies cried out furiously as Zeus raged in a thunderous tantrum. Clouds hovered over Ares, flickering as he kneeled in front of the storm, cowering like a child being scolded. The cloud of fury looked down at his son in disappointment. "You had almost a week to find them, yet you have failed to return the fallen Gods to me. And why? Because you'd been comatose by two mortals? Pathetic!"

Thunder echoed through the throne room, making the hairs on the back of Ares' neck stand up. He looked up at his father, his eyes wide with fear as he stuttered through his words. "F-forgive me, Father, th-they tricked me!"

Zeus's voice swallowed Ares' pleas. "Silence!" He speared a lightning bolt right by Ares' knees, knocking him back. The God of War whimpered.

Zeus continued bitterly. "I should've known not to send you. You've always been nothing but a disappointment to me, Ares." The shadow of storm clouds engulfed itself over Ares. "It just goes to show…" The clouds slowly morphed to the appearance of the large, muscle-bound god. His voice rose past the vaulted ceilings. "If you want something done right..." Zeus scowled down at Ares. "You have to do it yourself." The towering king began to walk out of his throne room. "The time of the fallen Gods is over. I'll kill Hermes and Apollo myself. Who knows, I might just wipe out humanity as well." Zeus turned and looked down at Ares sniveling on the ground. He gestured his head at Ares to follow him. "Come, boy, you might learn a thing or two."

Ares got himself to his feet. He looked at Artemis in her cage, who was smirking at him mockingly. She began to whisper. "Little Ares. So desperate for his daddy's approval. I pity you."

Ares walked up to the cage, glaring at Artemis. He hissed back. "You pity me, yet you're the one in a cage."

Artemis stared back at Ares. She grabbed onto the bars of the cage, leaning closer towards him, staring at him intensely. "Keep telling yourself that, brother." Artemis snickered at her brother. "You realize you will never be enough for him, don't you?"

Ares clenched his teeth at her. "You disrespectful little—"

Thunder rumbled impatiently in the distance. The stern echo of Zeus's voice followed. "Ares, come!"

Ares quickly looked back towards Zeus. He stared back at Artemis before timidly following his father out of the throne room.

Artemis gazed out at the night sky from the opening in the throne room. "By the Gods, please hurry..." she said.

***

Down below, Hermes and Lance walked by the beach under the stars. They held hands as they watched the waves coast by. "I've never stopped long enough to notice how beautiful the ocean can be." Hermes said to Lance.

Lance chuckled. "That's why I moved here."

Hermes stared at Lance endearingly. He spoke softly to his lover. "I suppose it is a view worth moving for."

Lance looked back curiously. "So why'd you move here? Greece sounds like an amazing place to live."

Hermes looked down. "I suppose it is…"

Lance noticed Hermes's shift in demeanor. He put a hand on his cheek. "Sorry if I brought up a sore subject…"

Hermes smiled weakly. "You're okay. It's nothing I haven't already been thinking about."

Lance grabbed Hermes' hands gently, looking worried. "Everything okay?"

Hermes sighed, tired of carrying on his charade. "I have to tell you something. It's going to sound absurd to you."

Lance gave Hermes an assuring smile. "You can tell me anything; I'm not going to judge you."

Hermes took another deep breath in. "I've lied to you about who I am."

Lance gazed wide-eyed. "Oh god, you have a wife."

Hermes blinked, raising a confused eyebrow.

"What? No, no, nothing like that." Hermes grew nervous, tugging at the collar of his shirt.

Lance leaned closer. "Then what is it? Who are you?"

Hermes sighed and looked back at Lance with a serious expression on his face. "I'm Hermes, Messenger of the Gods. My brother is Apollo, God of the Sun. We were turned mortal and cast down from Olympus by our father Zeus."

Lance stood frozen in shock. "You're fucking with me, right?"

Hermes stared back at him, straight-faced. "I told you it would sound absurd."

Lance chuckled, humoring his lover. "Okay, then, well, if you really are the former Messenger of the Gods, then prove it. Can't you fly?"

Hermes grinned widely. "Oh, that's easy!" Hermes quickly grabbed Lance tightly by the waist, pulling him close.

"What are you—" Lance screamed as Hermes suddenly ascended with him fifty feet or so into the sky. Wind blew in their faces as they tasted the clouds. Lance stopped screaming, now only able to look at Hermes with a dumbfounded expression. "Holy shit!" He exclaimed.

Hermes smirked smugly as he gripped Lance close to his chest.

After the initial shock wore off, Hermes told Lance everything. How he planned to overthrow his father, restore their godhood, and even his doubts about it. It would be a lot for anyone to take in, though to Hermes' surprise, Lance took it remarkably well. Hermes and Lance sat on top of the Ferris wheel at the pier, looking out at the coastline.

"Wow… Your dad sounds like a dick," Lance stated matter-of-factly.

Hermes agreed somberly. "Indeed."

Lance chuckled in disbelief before muttering to himself. "I'm sleeping with Hermes, Messenger of the Gods."

His lover nodded, though he corrected Lance. "Former Messenger of the Gods."

"Not for long…" Lance paused, "Why are you telling me all of this? I mean, I'm just another mortal, right? Pretty soon you'll forget all about me."

Hermes hugged Lance, kissing him on the forehead. "Not at all, darling. In the month I've been here, I've felt more alive than the eons I lived as a god, all because of you. You've shown me what it means to be mortal." Hermes smiled softly. "Have you ever heard the tale of Eros and Psyche?"

Lance shrugged. "I don't think so."

The former God continued to do what he did best: tell a story. "To make a long story short, it's about a mortal and a god falling in love, and despite all the odds, they live happily ever after."

Hermes looked into Lance's eyes. "I'm telling you all this because that's what I want for us. I'm in love with you, Lance. I want to live happily ever after with you."

The timid mortal still seemed on the fence. "I love you too, but…"

Hermes' brow crinkled. "But what?"

Lance sighed. "Look, that story is sweet and all, but my life is down here, Hermes. And pretty soon you'll be back in Olympus, busy with godly things more important than me."

Hermes put a hand on Lance's cheek. "What if I wasn't a God then?"

Lance looked surprised. "Oh, really? You'd pass up the chance to be a God again for me?"

"I love you so much I'd happily live and die as a mortal with you." He persisted.

Lance let out a soft, glossy-eyed smile. "Do you really mean that?" His voice cracked, choking back tears of joy.

Hermes nodded as he began to tear up as well. "More than anything."

The two kissed passionately on top of the roof. Holding each other as if it were the last time they'd do so. They laid back and looked at the stars. Lance rested his head atop Hermes' chest.

Hermes looked back at Lance and gestured to the stars. "I bet some day you'll be up there."

Lance looked at the night sky. "Up where? In the stars?"

Hermes nodded. "The Gods would honor those they deemed heroes by casting them among the stars. The greatest of all fates. Just like Eros and Psyche."

Lance chuckled. "And how am I a hero?"

Hermes looked down and smiled at Lance. "You've taught empathy to the Gods."

They stayed up on top of the Ferris wheel for hours just enjoying each other's company. It felt like their own peaceful little world.

***

Later that night, Hermes went home to break the bad news to his brother. Thunder and lightning flashed and echoed outside the apartment window as Hermes walked inside to see Apollo packing some things into a box.

Hermes questioned Apollo defensively. "What are you doing?"

Apollo replied as he loaded various items into a cardboard box. "Well, seeing it's the end of the month and Artemis will be here any day now, I figured I'd pack a few souvenirs to bring back to Olympus. Anything you want me to pack for you?"

Hermes scratched the back of his head. "I don't think so, brother…"

Apollo continued to put trinkets into the box. "Oh, come on, how about that VHS player you're so fond of?"

Hermes cleared his throat. "I don't think I'm going back, brother."

Apollo paused, looking at Hermes in disbelief. "You're not coming back? I—I don't understand…"

"I'm going to stay here and live and die as a mortal. It's what I want."

Apollo stood up, waving a stack of CDs around angrily, before throwing them across the room. "You're not making sense, brother. It's what you want? How could you not want to be a God?"

"Because living down here for a month has been more of a life than being a God ever was! I've learned so much living among them! Hurting as they do, loving as they do—"

Apollo rolled his eyes and cut Hermes off. "Oh, by the Gods, this is about Lance? Would you really trade immortality for a piece of ass?"

Hermes persisted in trying to convince his brother, though, to no avail. "It's not like that, I love him!"

Apollo ignored his brother's feelings. "Brother! There will be plenty of other mortals to fuck!"

Hermes stared at his brother in disappointment. He lowered his voice. "You still don't get it. You've spent a month walking in their shoes, yet you still can't seem to empathize with them. Mortals are just as important as the Gods. With what they've done, what they've felt, all without our aid, we should be the ones worshiping them."

Apollo stared glossy-eyed at Hermes. "You want me to empathize when you're the one abandoning your brother?" Apollo's voice began to shake. "You said you were stuck with me…"

"Apollo, I…"

Three heavy thuds, each harsher than the last shook the front door. Apollo and Hermes froze. Thunder cracked from the hallway. The door hinges rattled before the door snapped from its frame, flying through the living room and onto the two brothers, pinning them to the ground. They groaned and looked up to see their father standing in the doorway with Ares. Zeus stepped into the apartment. "My two forgotten sons." Zeus grinned menacingly. "Did you miss your father?"

CHAPTER 11
DADDY DEAREST

THUNDER ROARED THROUGH the skies of Mount Olympus as Artemis waited anxiously in her cage in her father's throne room. Lightning struck outside the window of the palace as a raven flew past it, narrowly avoiding being electrocuted. The raven swooped in and landed on Artemis's cage, dropping the jar of nightshade into her hands.

Artemis sighed in relief. "By the Gods, they actually did it!" Artemis stuck her fingers out of the top of the cage to pet the raven. "Well done, my darling."

A voice echoed from the throne room entrance— Athena stood in the doorway, holding a golden key. "Was the harvest fruitful?" Artemis turned to see her sister Athena walking towards her.

"Indeed," Artemis replied as she proudly held up the jar of berries.

Athena smiled and nodded her head back at Artemis. "Excellent." The smile on Athena's face quickly faded to a look of urgency as she unlocked the cage for Artemis. "Father is flying down now; it should be mere minutes before he finds them, if he hasn't already…"

Artemis stretched her back. "We mustn't keep them waiting." Artemis whistled loudly with her two fingers, manifesting two griffins out of thin air. The creatures let out a hell-raising sound that was a cross between the roar of a lion and the screech of an eagle before bowing towards the Goddesses. Artemis turned towards her sister, looking hopeful as they mounted the ethereal steeds. "Tell me, sister, are you ready to overthrow the God of Gods?"

Athena stared back eagerly; a warrior's fire burned deep in her eyes. "I've been waiting millennia for someone to ask me that."

The two soared down from Olympus, across the restless tides, as they raced against the rising sun towards Los Angeles.

***

Back in Los Angeles, it seemed as if the fates had woven a thread for the worst.

"I must say, I've never been one for family reunions…" Zeus chuckled as he held a bloody-faced Hermes by the throat in the center of the apartment. Ares dropped a nearly unconscious Apollo on the floor in front of his father. Zeus scowled down at Hermes as

87

his eyes flickered with electricity. "You two were my favorite sons, you know…" Hermes gasped for air as he struggled to break free from his father's iron grip. Zeus continued. "I suppose that's why I showed you mercy even after you disobeyed me. I even let you live among the vermin you love so much… Yet you repay me by staging a coup against me?" Hermes choked as his father's hand gripped tighter around his neck. Zeus smiled thunderously. "This time you can forget about mercy. You will die as all mortals do."

Hermes struggled as his father's hold turned fatally tight. Though before Zeus could kill Hermes, a frying pan hit him on the head, falling to the floor dented. He looked up to see Lance staring back at him, terrified, though holding his ground. Lance's voice shook. "Let —let h-him go!"

Hermes looked at Lance and frantically back at Zeus. Still gasping for air, he began to beg his father. "Please… don't…"

Zeus chuckled before dropping Hermes to the floor. He walked over to Lance. "My, my, well, don't you look like a young Ganymede!" Zeus turned back to Hermes, who was panting on the floor. "Is this your concubine, son?" He gestured at Lance, who stood petrified.

"Don't hurt him… I'm begging you." Hermes choked.

Zeus rolled his eyes. "You've become too attached to these things. That's all they are really, just things. Little trinkets Gods use to pass the time." Zeus stroked Lance's ghostly pale face before grabbing him by it and hurling him out the window.

Hermes let out a bloodied scream of agony, dropping his head, sobbing hysterically.

"Quit your sniveling, boy. It's pathetic. Face your demise with at least a sliver of honor." Zeus sneered.

Blood and tears dripped from Hermes's face as he looked up at his father. "What do you know about honor?"

Zeus smirked before backhanding Hermes to the ground. Hermes winced in pain. Zeus grinned devilishly. "Look how frail you've become. Your humanity has made you weak, boy."

Hermes stood up, staring at his father with rage-filled eyes. "Mortals aren't weak… and I think you know that. All they've achieved without your help. You feel threatened, don't you?"

Lightning lashed Hermes like a whip, charring his blood-soaked blazer and hurling him to the floor. Zeus yelled impatiently. "Enough!" He looked furiously at his son. His eyes twitched as lightning flickered throughout them. He began to rise into the air, forming a storm around the room. "Such absurdity. The Gods fearing mortals? I will not tolerate disrespect! You will die for your insolence…" Zeus looked down, smiling psychotically at Hermes. "But not before you watch every last mortal perish!" Zeus expanded into his true divine form, bursting through the roof with a roar of thunder. The storm circulating around the apartment quickly shifted to a hurricane spreading throughout Venice. The clouds blackened. Floodwaters surged through the streets, swallowing cars and people alike. Blasted from their crumbling apartment, Hermes and

Apollo lay unconscious on the beach. Zeus loomed above them, now twenty feet tall. "Time for humanity to end once and for all!" The God of the Sky's voice howled like a gust of wind.

Humanity had reached its darkest hour. Though in the midst of the darkness, a golden light shone through the storm, revealing two glowing Goddesses. Artemis and Athena soared down by griffin-back, rushing towards Zeus. The creatures screeched and growled as they dodged lightning strikes. Athena shouted to Artemis. "I'll go down low and distract him while you fly up and wait for an opening." Athena looked at her sister with both fear and faith. "You've got one shot at this, sister. Make it count." Athena flew down to Zeus' feet, stabbing her freshly sharpened golden sword into the nail bed of his big toe. "I hope this hurts!" She cried out.

Zeus yowled out in pain. Artemis pulled back her bow, aiming it at her father's open mouth. "I guess you don't see everything..." With one shot, Artemis delivered the arrow fated to slay the King of Gods. The nightshade landed perfectly placed in the back of her father's throat. Zeus grabbed his neck, making a gagging sound before falling back and causing a small tremor in the process. His twenty-foot frame lay unconscious across the sand of Venice Beach before he slowly began to shrink to the size of a mortal.

Athena stood beside her father's body and proceeded to cut off two of his fingers. She stared back at him for a moment. "It's finally over..." she said to herself in disbelief.

Artemis flew down by her, landing on the beach. "We're not finished yet! Give me the fingers!"

Athena tossed Artemis the fingers and proceeded to chop up the rest of her father, sealing his remains in a golden sack. Artemis flew off towards her brothers. Apollo stood protectively in front of Hermes, who was still unconscious. Ares laughed maniacally as he cornered his brothers. "This is the end, brother."

Just then Artemis swept down on her griffin, dropping one of their father's fingers to Apollo. Artemis' voice echoed back as she flew up into the air again. "Eat it!"

Ares rushed at Apollo, though he quickly swallowed the finger and began to glow gold. An explosion of light knocked back Ares. Apollo walked towards him now wearing his godly armor, radiating with divinity once again. He picked up Ares by the straps of his armor. "Don't forget what happened at the Olympics, bitch." Apollo knocked Ares unconscious. He smirked as the Trojan God rag-dolled across the sand.

Artemis rode back down, jumping off her horse and hugging her brother tightly. "Thank the Gods you're okay!"

Apollo nodded endearingly. "Thanks to you, sister."

Artemis smiled at her brother before looking back to where Hermes was, seeing he was gone. "Where's Hermes?" she questioned.

Apollo looked off in the distance to see his brother kneeling by a body on the beach. Apollo turned to Artemis. "Give me a moment." Apollo approached his brother to see him cradling Lance's lifeless, mangled body in his arms.

Hermes sobbed silently as he stroked Lance's battered face gently. "I swear by the Gods I'll put you in the stars…" Hermes clutched him closely, dripping tears onto him. He kissed him gently goodbye on the forehead before breaking down again.

Apollo kneeled down next to Hermes and placed a hand on his shoulder. Hermes hung his head against his brother. Apollo held him tightly, consoling him as he wept into his arms.

CHAPTER 12
THE THEFT OF APOLLO'S CATTLE

IT WAS EONS ago. A time when Nymphs still roamed the lush, evergreen meadows of Mount Cyllene. The Earth was untouched. Still pure and innocent to the countless wars that would stain its soil. Flowers bloomed from the Earth with no worry of ever being picked. Crisp mountain peaks framed the coastline, their shadows stretching over the fields with just the right touch of shade. Sunlight shimmered across the crystalline blue waters of Lake Doxa. Cattle roamed through the fields, eating grass or leisurely napping under oak trees. It was a serene place for all who inhabited it. Even the cow with a chunk of his abdomen cut out seemed to be unbothered given all things considered. Solitude's blissful silence tiptoed gracefully across the plains, though all of a sudden, winds began to cry out in a harsh and unforgiving howl. The ominous wail quickly ascended to an unnerving rumble. Lightning flickered in the sky as the crack of its bolt echoed down in a menacing chorus of fury.

A single, concentrated ray of sunlight beamed down from the heavens, scorching the fields and sending the cattle into a panicked frenzy. As the lingering blindness faded, a broad-shouldered figure emerged, walking swiftly through the smoldering wake. A Divine aura radiated from him. His platinum blond hair clashed against bronzed skin, a golden laurel wreath proudly nestled into his shimmering locks. He sported a short red robe complemented by a golden bow and quiver of arrows snuggly secured to his back. He muttered to himself, enraged as he stomped through the hoard of screeching cows. "Steal my cattle, why don't you? Haven't you any clue who I am? I'm the God of Light for Zeus's sake! Oh I'll show you... you..." Just then Apollo, the God of Light, was stopped in his tracks by a sight that would dumbfound all of Olympus. A small infant stood before the God of the Sun, unapologetically eating a cooked fillet of meat which used to be part of one of Apollo's favorites out of his cattle.

"Well hello, traveler." Despite his age, the infant greeted the God with a bold charisma, grubbily shoving the hunk of cooked meat up into his face. "Care for a bite?"

"You insolent bug," Apollo began to glow with the heat of his words, flames licking the ground below his feet, flickering about his frame. He hissed his words through clenched teeth. "That cattle you're eating belongs to me!"

"Well…" The infant began, hardly acknowledging this fit of anger, still gnawing away at the hunk of meat. He leisurely finished his bite before addressing the towering deity, who scowled down at him. "You really should make sure they are fed a well-balanced diet. It has a bit of a gamey taste to it. You are what you eat after all."

The fire grew to a roar, flames feeding off the fuming God. His hair engulfed into a bright flame nearly shooting into the sky. He shook with rage as he stared down at the child. "You better explain to me why one of my cows has a chunk of his abdomen missing or so help me I will skin you alive!"

The infant nonchalantly finished off the last bit of cooked cow, beginning to explain himself in between bites. "Easy there, my glowing golden friend. I have a perfectly reasonable explanation for eating your cattle. Which I cooked perfectly might I add."

Apollo hovered over him with his arms folded like a parent scolding their child, Apollo gave the boy a cold and unforgiving death stare. "I'm waiting."

The infant mischievously put his hands out and shrugged. "I was hungry." He grinned at the still fiery Apollo, as if he had no idea the God could fry him at any given second. He proceeded to explain his story with a tone that indicated it wasn't at all his fault. "You see, after being born only a few hours ago, not a pleasant experience I might add, I required a bit of protein to sustain myself so I wouldn't perish from starvation. And in all fairness, your cattle were out in the open ripe for the taking." He innocently gestured his head to the partially butchered livestock.

Apollo's anger quickly shifted to bewilderment. He tilted his head in confusion. "You... were just born? And yet you can speak, cook and..."

"Entertain?" Just then the infant reached behind him, pulling out what would famously become the lyre. Though at this stage, its design was purely practical. The lyre was made out of the curved rib bone of one of the cattle and the strings were a sliver of intestine. To be fair, the infant thought he didn't do a half bad job at making it look somewhat aesthetically pleasing. He grinned widely as he tantalizingly dangled the instrument in the God's face.

At first the God found no interest in whatever trinket he was holding. He flared his nostrils in distaste at the smugly bold child. "I was going to say steal...," he hissed.

The infant chuckled mischievously at the God's words. "Perhaps a song will lighten the mood!" Hermes gripped the end of the lyre, about to play.

Apollo began to protest. "Don't think you can get out of this by..." Though with one strum of the lyre, his cold heartless death stare faded and began to grow into a wide-eyed gaze of child-like wonderment. "In all my chariot rides, I've never heard something more beautiful. Please, please, young one! Keep playing, don't stop!"

The infant continued to effortlessly pick the strings of the instrument as he spoke. "Oh this old thing? I was bored a few hours ago so I managed to fashion this out of one of your cattle. Once again, I do apologize for that. As a matter of fact, why don't you have this as a gift? Consider it reparations. I'll even throw in a free lesson if you're interested."

He muted the strings with his palm before handing the lyre over to Apollo, who strummed a single chord and began to giggle with excitement.

"This is quite remarkable craftsmanship! You have yourself a deal!" The God grinned, "You know, I may have misjudged you, my small infantile friend." He plucked his fingers across each string, entranced by the instrument in his hands. Though, in all the excitement running through his head, one important question managed to surface. "I must say I'm quite curious, what parents would birth such a prodigy?" He cocked his eyebrow up and turned to the oddly charming baby.

The infant blew hot air onto his nails, polishing them against an all too comfortable-looking cattle-skin robe. "Oh why Zeus the God of the Skies is my father. My mother, Maia, tells me I'm one of his many infidelities." He spoke with a shrug of his shoulders and tut of his chin, capitalizing his disinterested tone.

Apollo looked up from the lyre and at the completely self-reliant infant, finishing the last bits of his steak by the fire he started. "That makes sense…" The infant smirked at the lack of shock in the God's voice.

"I suppose you'd be my brother, Apollo, the God of the Sun?" He looked up from his meal and back at the glowing deity.

"As well as the God of Music." Apollo began strumming the lyre with a familiarity that spoke more to his domain than his words. "So what is your name, fellow son of Zeus?"

The infant gave a bow that tiptoed on the line between elegant and condescending. "My name's Hermes, it's a pleasure to formally meet you, Apollo."

Chuckling lightly, Apollo found himself more than amused by Hermes' charming though mischievous nature. Although, his enjoyment hinged heavily on the fact that the boy reminded him of himself in his younger years. "Well Hermes, why don't you come with me to Olympus? I think father is going to want to meet you."

Hermes shot a devilish grin back at the God. "Who am I to keep the family waiting? Let us go then, brother!" Hermes ran ahead of Apollo, waving at him to hurry up.

Apollo smirked. "I must say, I like you much more than some of the other siblings."

CHAPTER 13
TO BE HUMAN

AND JUST LIKE that, it was all over. The siblings cleaned up what they could of the ruin Zeus left behind in Venice. Lightning scorched the sands to glass. Buildings along the boardwalk had been smashed to mere nails and drywall. Artemis called upon an army of doves to gather up the bodies scattered about the glass beach, providing them a burial at sea. Lance was the last to be sent off, coins placed in his eyes offering him safe passage.

One might wonder how humanity would react to discovering the existence of Gods, though fortunately, the Gods didn't have to worry about this. Whether it was the design of the fates or just a morbid case of luck, Zeus killed all eyewitnesses of the attack. Those who were indoors for the storm that almost ended humanity hardly noticed the event due to their fixation on a breaking news story coinciding with the attack. The story followed the trial of a professional football player turned actor, accused of murdering his ex-wife.

To the siblings' surprise, Venice was quickly restored to its former glory with the aid of their maimed brother. Hephaestus, now with a pair of cybernetic eyes and metal claws for hands, came down eager to test his new inventions. The magnified scopes sticking out of his face casted a pale green glow similar to a computer screen, illuminating a prideful smile, foreign to the God. He stood tall for the first time in eons, hammering away towards something greater. One must never underestimate the God of the Forge.

Artemis and Athena finished strapping the bag of their father's remains to the back of one of the griffins. Apollo and Hermes stood next to them, bidding farewell.

"So what now?" Apollo questioned his sisters as if it were the first time he'd really thought about it.

Artemis replied. "We'll take Father to Tartarus where he will be imprisoned with his father, Kronos. Then we rebuild. Father damaged Gaia greatly by neglecting her; it'll take time and all the Gods we can get, but we'll fix it."

Apollo nodded to Artemis. "Sister, thank you. For everything. I don't know how I can ever begin to repay you."

Artemis playfully punched her brother on the shoulder. "You can start by helping me clean up this mess."

Artemis and Athena climbed atop their winged

steeds. Athena turned to Hermes. "By the way, this is for you, Hermes." Athena reached into the bag of her father's remains, pulling out a finger and tossing it to Hermes, who reluctantly caught it. She spoke in a melancholic tone. "For if you change your mind. The Gods will miss you in your absence."

Hermes nodded at Athena and to Artemis as well. "Thank you, both of you, for everything."

Artemis and Athena nodded back before the griffins spread their wings and launched into the air, disappearing into the clouds. Apollo and Hermes stood on the glass-riddled beach, overlooking the ocean.

Apollo turned to Hermes, looking as if he already knew the answer to what he was about to ask. "So you're really going to stay?"

Hermes sighed assuredly. "I am. I've lived and felt more here than I ever had on Olympus. I know it might seem foolish to you, but there's so much beauty in humanity. So much to learn from them. I can't just walk away from it."

Apollo tried his best to muster up a smile as he looked into his brother's eyes. "It's okay, brother. I understand now."

Hermes nodded, his eyes welling as he smiled softly back at his big brother. "Promise me you won't forget about mortals. Teach the gods to treat them with compassion. Don't look down upon them, look towards them for help. You can do what father couldn't. So much good could come of it."

Apollo nodded to his brother as he put a hand on his shoulder. "I promise you, brother. And I promise to honor Lance as well. Life is precious, eternal or not"

Tears streamed down Hermes' face. "Thank you."

Apollo, seeing his brother cry, couldn't help but do the same. "I—I should be thanking you for putting up with me for all these ages."

The two both chuckled through their sniveling, embracing the bittersweet end of their journey.

"I'm going to miss you." Hermes' voice shook as he spoke in between sobs.

Apollo wiped the wet streaks from his cheeks, only for more to come falling down. "I'll miss you too, brother."

They hugged each other tightly, dampening each other's shoulders. The brothers held their embrace as long as they could, neither one of them wanting to let go.

Apollo broke the silence. "Oh, I almost forgot!" He pulled out a pair of sunglasses, handing them to Hermes. "Could you hold onto these for me? I won't be needing them now, though I'll have to look stylish for the next bicentennial visit."

Hermes took the sunglasses, putting them into the pocket of his coat. He smiled, "I'll be looking forward to it." Then, Hermes reached into his coat and pulled out Zeus's finger, glancing at it, momentarily. "I suppose I won't be needing this…" He wound his arm back to throw it in the ocean, though Apollo stopped him.

Apollo grabbed his wrist, urging him not to. "Why don't you hold onto it? You know, just in case you change your mind."

Hermes looked incredibly sure of himself. "I won't." He replied.

Apollo put a hand over Hermes, lowering the finger. "Well, then just hold onto it as a favor for me, please. Think of it as a final souvenir." He smiled earnestly.

Hermes nodded and put the finger back in his pocket. He clicked his tongue reluctantly. "Well… I guess this is it then."

Tears shimmered off the God of Light's face; he was going to miss his old chum. Though he was still happy for his brother, as he knew in his heart it was what he wanted. He wiped the somber mist from his eyes. "I suppose so." He began to rise off the ground, ascending towards the heavens once again. He shouted down at his dearest brother in reassurance. "Don't worry though, I'll be sure to check in on you. Remember, you're stuck with me." He winked at Hermes, casting his signature prideful smirk one final time. The God looked down across the beach, which he'd admittedly come to think of as home. He fondly inhaled the salty breeze and everlasting scent of cigarettes below before shooting off into space. The glowing deity disappeared into the fading night sky, leaving a trail of stars behind him. The stars, which shined brighter than the rest, formed a new constellation, one in the shape of Lance.

Hermes looked up at the constellation of his fallen lover and smiled in remembrance. He stared up at the stars until the sunrise started to peek up from the coastline. The former God pulled out his brother's sunglasses from his coat, putting them on as he walked down the sidewalk. Feeling both the pain of loss as well as the joy of newfound hope, Hermes embraced the journey that is humanity with open arms. He walked past a radio left behind from Zeus's wreckage; Dreams by the Cranberries played statically through its speaker.

ABOUT THE AUTHOR

Tate Dousette is a speculative fiction author with a passion for mythology and modern storytelling. He has written a variety of short stories in fantasy and science fiction, and continues to expand his body of work. Tate lives in Mesa, Arizona with his cat, Gwenevere and too many roommates.